Why?

by

Kevin Crilly

This book is published by
Grosvenor House Publishing Ltd
28-30 High Street, Guildford, Surrey, GU1 3HY.
www.grosvenorhousepublishing.co.uk

A CIP record for this book
is available from the British Library

ISBN 978-1-906645-38-0

I dedicate this book to Babs.

She was the first person to read my script.

It was her excitement that spurred me on.

She is someone who has the right to complain, but never does.

Chapter One

Dave 1998

Standing in his cell looking out of the window, slowly swaying from side to side, the warm suns rays catching his eyes past the iron bars, he was starting to get angry with himself at spending all this time in here when he could have been with his lovely family. He started thinking about the past and his wife, Lynn, who had always stood by him, whatever he had done or wherever he had ended up. A beautiful girl, very proud of her family, and always looks a million dollars, not because of how much she spends on clothes, but the way she wears her old ones. She has never had much money, so would always take good care of the things she had. Her real name is Linda but her three children always call her Lynn, or Mum most of the time. Samantha and Charlotte, sixteen-year-old twin girls, and Dan, their older brother by one year.

Charlotte, or Charlie as she likes to be called, has long blonde hair; big brown eyes and looks just like her Mum, with the same personality, very friendly, outgoing and loves to talk!

Samantha has beautiful long white-blonde hair, sharp blue eyes and looks like her Dad a bit, not quite so outgoing as her sister. Like her Dad she doesn't mind her own company especially when she is writing her music or playing her guitar, but can be a right fruitcake when she gets going!

Dan was just like his Dad, a big lump! He could charm the pants off any girl with just one of his smiles! Lynn was bigger when she was pregnant with Dan than she was with the girls; the moment he popped out the nurses said he was going to be a right bruiser! Even at an early age Dan was very protective of his family, and doted on his sisters. Lynn loves them with every inch of her body and they would do everything together. Mainly clothes shopping if there was any spare money left after paying the bills, which was not that often, but window shopping was still good fun, although not for Dan. He was always being dragged around the shops with his sisters; all he ever said about shopping was what a waste of life and please let it end soon!

Lynn had a part-time job at the girls' school to help the teachers with the problem kids. She was a great talker and listener, a rare talent that can't be taught. Somehow, she could always manage to get the children to tell her all their troubles, even some of the teachers too! The extra money coming in was great, and she got to see her kids at the same time, which is probably the real reason why she took the job.

She never seemed to have time for herself. There was always so much to do, entertaining the girls' friends, who seemed to be at our house most nights. Even after school she would give up her time to help out with all sorts, netball, or football. The football must have been funny to watch, as she knows absolutely nothing about the game! The boys would be kicking each other as well as the ball and she probably thought it was part of the rules!

Taking Dan to rugby a couple of times a week wasn't too bad, the small club he played for was just a short walk away. They would go through a park and then through open woodlands, but it was a beautiful place and there were normally three or four other mums and their kids to walked with them, so there was always someone to talk to.

One of the dads had built a shed just by the side of the pitch out of bits of wood he 'borrowed' off the building sites he worked on. It didn't look very pretty and the front part was missing, but it kept the wind and rain out, just!

As soon as all the boys were settled and the trainer had control of them, the mums would park themselves on the white plastic garden chairs, open up their flasks of piping hot tea, then watch the boys roll about on the floor and cover their lovely clean clothes in mud! A couple of the mums would have a little moan now and then, "Bloody hell! I've only just washed and ironed all that kit!" But they would always have a bit of a laugh and try to put the world to rights at the same time.

Dan's boxing club was a 10 minute bus ride away, but only once a week for this one. It was in an old rundown building just behind a working men's club, which was just off the council estate. Dan loved the place, it wasn't very big, and the small amount of equipment they had was old, but it did the job, and it was always spotless. Dan said part of the discipline training was to keep the gym clean and tidy at all times. Lynn wished he would bring the message home with him; his room was always a bloody mess!

Bert was the lovely old guy who ran the club on a shoestring, and probably used some of his own money as well. He wasn't very tall but quite stocky, very clean cut, with a nose that was nearly as wide as his face from too many fights! Apparently he has had just as many punch-ups outside the ring as inside! Bert was as fit as a fiddle, and would still go a few rounds with anyone who challenged him. He didn't drink or smoke and still had a bit of a reputation, even at the age of 62. He was your 'no nonsense' type, very strict but fair, and he was great with the kids, a good role model for them to look up to, although they didn't have to look up too far! But they all liked and respected him.

Bert said Dan was a natural boxer, and after only a few months of training, he was able to put up a good fight in the ring. Lynn would drop him off and have a walk around the shopping centre that was just up the road. Sometimes Dan would ask her to stay and watch him go a couple of rounds with another boy, but she could only watch him boxing with one eye covered up by her hand and the other eye half closed in a squint looking through the fingers of her other hand, just in case her little boy got hurt! But, just like his Dad, it was normally the other people that came off worse. Dave was able to take Dan to the club now and then, and he would help Bert out in any way he could. Not just with money but with his time as well, knowing how important these little clubs were for the kids.

Lynn has helped out on numerous school trips, which she would always volunteer for, and most of the kids would always ask if she was going with them. Never again, however, would she go on a school trip that meant setting one foot on a boat or ferry! That is definitely off Lynn's curriculum!

The boat trip to France had been quite uneventful at first. It was a nice sunny day but quite cold. A few kids were running about, but they were just excited and doing no harm that Lynn could see. She got herself a cup of hot strong tea from the tuck shop (bloody expensive it was, too!) and she parked herself down on a seat she found in a corner, away from most people and out of the chilly wind. She took a couple of sips of tea, then tilted her head back against the boat and turned it slightly until it rested against the bright orange life ring. She closed her eyes for a bit. The warm sun on her face soon made her relax, and she drifted into a little world of her own. The noise of the children and the other passengers slowly faded away, and soon all she could hear was the sea splashing up the side of the hull. The boat moved with what seemed like very little effort through the water, the vibration of the engines gently massaging her body through the cold steel...Thoughts of Dave came flooding back...

A violent man, she knows that, but he has never once used his immense strength, or violence, against her or the children. She sometimes wonders where his reputation comes from. Lynn knows her family is always safe when Dave's around. Even when he's in prison his friends are always ready to help, no question.

Dave would do the same, and has done in the past, when his mates have been 'out of town' at Her Majesty's Pleasure! Still in a world of her own, she started to think about the first time she saw Dave. He was a bouncer at a nightclub she used to go to. Lynn and her mates were standing in the long queue, which never moved fast enough, but as they got closer to the front this new doorman just seemed to stand out. Not a model by any means, he was about six foot tall and very stocky with short blond hair, and definitely not what your Mum would want you to bring home! But just because he couldn't waddle down a catwalk didn't mean he was ugly! He had a charm about him; smart, confident and you could see he liked the ladies. As the queue moved slowly forward you could hear him telling people very politely;

"This way... that way.... don't do that... keep the noise down.... sorry Gents, not tonight."

"How can someone look so hard, and be so polite?" she thought to herself. She couldn't take her eyes off him! Lynn didn't go for the pretty 'I love myself' boys; she preferred the rugged type; more the guy who built the catwalk, rather than the one who prances down it! Not dirty or scruffy, the sort of rugby type. Rough, but cleans up well!

Lynn always had the pick of most men in the club; tall, blonde, legs that go on forever, and a sexy smile. They were all having a good time. Friday night was always a ball. Some old chit chat about work, who was having an affair with whom, any young men started work at your place, how much bloody money the boss makes, and how little he gives you!

Lynn worked in a builder's merchant for a while, maybe that's why she liked the rough type. Always laughing and joking, none of them could be serious, they would come out with the same old bullshit time and time again, but it made the days go much quicker. Meeting and dealing with all those builders made her realise that what you see is what you get. Sometimes you would get so called 'builders' in the shop that were up to no good, the gypsies or travellers, as they liked to be called. The local gypsies were OK as long as they thought they were getting a good deal, the ones passing through were not always so nice.

One or two yard staff always followed them in ready to give her some support if they got out of hand. Any regular customers that were in the shop at the same time would always hang around until they went on their way. Nothing was ever said by the builders or yard staff, but most left with a reassuring smile, and she knew they would help if she ever needed it.

Chapter Two

Lynn 1980

The drinks we'd had in the pub were starting to take effect now, and all the silly talk and giggles were beginning to flow. The group of boys in front of us must have had a good drink too; you could tell by the way they were acting; they were so loud, which was a bit silly, as we were only about twenty feet from the door staff. I could see one of the bouncers having a quick look every now and then, to make sure they weren't going too far. The whole queue moved up a bit more; just these boys in front, and then it would be our turn. As they walked forward to the door, one of the bouncers said,

"Sorry lads, not tonight," which didn't surprise me. Then it started;

"Come on mate, do us a favour it's Friday night!"

"Sorry lads," he said again, "you've had too much to drink."

"Oh for fuck's sake! We've stood in this fucking queue, freezing fucking cold for ages! What's wrong with us?" Boys with drink in them are so stupid; swearing at the door staff makes your chances of getting in zero.

"Time to go lads, time to go." The bouncer unhooked the thick rope that kept us all in line, then put one of his arms out to show them that they must go. But being polite is not working with these six lads. Keeping his eyes fixed on the boys, still being polite but minus the smile, he dropped the rope then worked his way in between them and us. He was trying to protect us from the lads, which was sort of working. He was a big guy and so was his mate, but... two against six! And they were not your normal whimpy looking boys.

'Get some more staff out here to help you,' I was thinking to myself. It was beginning to get very heated, more shouting, more swearing, and some pushing; they are not going without a fight. Then the doorman moved so quickly, I wasn't sure what happened, but the two boys who'd done the pushing were flat on their backs, out cold! Then he got straight back in between us and the other four lads who were still standing.

No more shouting, swearing or pushing, just silence. The two doormen stood still, just looking at them, but you could see they were ready for some more action if the lads wanted it. This guy was very good at his job, but maybe he went a bit too far this time, I thought. The four lads stood there for about 30 seconds, looking at their mates on the floor then up at the two doormen, they knew it was time to go. They picked their two mates up off the floor and just walked away without saying another word. Probably thinking to themselves; 'That was a quick night out!'

As soon as they were a safe distance away the doorman turned round to face me.

"Sorry girls, are you all OK?" He looked me straight in the eyes for my reaction, seeming almost embarrassed at what he had done in front of us. It was that look that told me he had a nice side to him as well, which made me feel even more attracted to him!

"Yes, we're OK," I said, with a little smile. He looked so relieved and went straight back to being 'Mister Nice And Polite,' "This way please... that way please... in you all go."

We finally made it into the club and got warmed up. Right! Time to have some fun! We all had a few more drinks, lots of dancing and a bit of flirting, just a good old Friday night out. It was my turn to buy a round of drinks, so off I went to the bar. There are always too many people waiting and not enough bar staff, so I got in the sort of queue and started 'people watching' for a bit. I had to smile to myself at the really drunk people trying their hardest not to act drunk, the people who can't dance trying to dance with some sort of rhythm, and all the boys trying to get off with the girls! Most of them stood no chance!

Tonight had a good feel about it, everyone seemed relaxed just wanting to enjoy themselves; even the bar staff were having fun tonight. The bouncers looked at ease too, standing well back and just letting the punters do their stuff. There was something different about the place tonight; it had a really good atmosphere. I was to find out why later. It was this new doorman with a fearsome reputation, no more scumbags in this club! If you do get in and cause trouble it won't be long before you find yourself out the back with a good kicking!

(He had a more cynical side to him as well. Had I known about it then, I might not have got involved with him.)

Then I spotted him; he was raised up slightly above everyone else so he had a good view of the whole dance floor. All of a sudden I realized he was looking straight at me and I felt a little tingle inside! What was it with this guy? I gave him a smile, he grinned back, the ultra violet light making his teeth glow whiter than white, then with a nod of his head he went back to watching the dance floor.

The night went well, no more trouble, just a few drunks escorted out, girls as well as boys. We got in the queue for our coats, which always turns into a mad scramble. Even with all the heat from inside the club you could feel the ice-cold breeze coming up the stairs from the front entrance. As we were leaving, he was back on the front door with a black scarf wrapped around his neck, which made him look even bigger!

"Goodnight," I could hear him saying, "Come back soon!" Some said "Goodbye." Some could hardly walk, and were being half carried out by their friends! As I walked through the doors I could see he was looking for someone. As soon as he saw me, he came straight over and asked me if I'd had a good time, giving me one of his lovely smiles.

"Yes thanks," I said.

"Are you coming back next week then?" he asked.

"Maybe," I said, with a bit of a flirty smile.

"Great!" he said, rubbing his hands together as if he had just won a prize! "No queuing for you or your mates, just come and see me as a special guest. What's your name then, darling?" he asked me, still with a great big grin on his face.

"Lynn and friends," I replied firmly. He laughed out loud and then said,

"OK, see you next week then!" As the week went on I kept thinking of him more and more. I didn't have a steady boyfriend at the moment but it didn't bother me too much, I had only just split up from my old boyfriend, who became a pain in the arse, and it was nice to be single for a while.

Friday came around and we all met at my parents' place, because it was the closest house to the bus stop. As we were all doing our final touches of make-up, my mates started teasing me, "Special guest! Special guest!"

We normally go to a different club every week but my friends said, "OK, just for you, we'll go back to Champs!"

Then again they all started chanting and pointing their fingers at me; "Special guest! Special guest!" trying to embarrass me. It was working!

As always, it was into the pub first for a few drinks, then on to the club. The queue to get in was a lot longer tonight, and it definitely wasn't warm.

" Come on!" they all kept saying, "its bloody cold out here! You're a special guest!"

"No, no, he might not remember me," I said, "let's just queue up with everyone else."

"No way!" said Ruth, and off she marched right up to the front and tapped the doorman on the shoulder! Ruth was always up front with everything she did and said, and always the life and soul of the party, but she also got us in trouble now and then with her big mouth! He turned around really quickly and went straight into defence mode, but as soon as he saw who it was he gave her a big smile,

"Hey, how you doing?" He looked over Ruth's shoulder and asked, "Is Lynn with you?"

"Yes," said Ruth.

"Great!" he said. "Go get her and the rest of your party and come to the front of the queue." Ruth walked back to us with her hands on her hips, swaying her bum from side to side with a cocky little smile on her face!

"Let's go!" she laughed. "That's how it's done!"

We trooped past the queue. All the girls with next to nothing on, their boobs spilling out of their tiny tops, some of them looking like they had no skirts on at all, they were so small! Their breath was turning into little clouds as it hit the cold air; probably talking about the same old gossip, as we did no doubt! There were all the lads without jackets on, pretending to be warm to try to impress the girls next to them! Unfortunately, their chattering teeth gave them away! You could hear some of the other punters moaning as we walked right to the front.

"We could get used to this!" we all said to each other. As we were paying he came up to me,

"Hi Lynn, how are you?" I was flattered that he'd remembered my name.

"Fine," I replied, "thanks for getting us in."

"No problem." There was a bit of an awkward silence.

"By the way, my name's Dave," he said. "Have a nice time tonight. I'll see you later then."

As the night went on we caught eye contact a few times, and smiled at each other.

"I wonder why he hasn't come over to talk to me," I said to Ruth.

"I don't think they're allowed to talk to the punters inside the club," she said, "especially the girls."

We had a great time again, the night went really quickly and it was soon time to go. I was a bit disappointed that Dave hadn't come over and spoken to me. I started thinking that maybe he didn't go for my type. It seemed like nearly every guy in the club had tried it on with me, but I wasn't interested!

We walked up the stairs to the front doors. I couldn't see him with all the people getting their coats, but I could hear him saying goodnight to everyone, and telling them to come again. As soon as he saw us he came over.

"Hello again," he said, "did you have a good time tonight? Sorry I didn't come and talk, we're not allowed to talk to the punters inside the club, especially the girls."

I looked over at Ruth. She mimed 'told you so!' with a childish grin!

"If you'd like to come out with me one night, give my mate outside your phone number," said Dave.

"OK" I said and we smiled at each other.

He turned away and was straight back in work mode. I went outside and asked his friend if he would take my number and give it to Dave.

"Aha, so you're the one he keeps talking about!" he laughed, and that made me feel a bit better. He gave me a wink and put my number in his pocket.

Dave phoned the next day, no awkward silence this time. He was a good talker, and a good listener; we were on the phone for ages. I asked him how come I hadn't seen him before, as we went to most clubs in the area. He told me that he looked after several clubs but not always on the same nights.

We went on a date and hit it off straight away. Every pub or club he took me to we went straight to the front, no queuing, just "Hello Dave, nice to see you mate," and a handshake. He would always introduce me to his friends and would never leave me out of the conversation, which made me feel very special, and they would always shake my hand. Some of his best mates would give me a kiss and a cuddle as well, just to wind Dave up, but never once did any of them take it any further than that. Most of them were big men and looked like animals, (they probably were!) but once you got to know them it became clear most of them were gentlemen, and they all had a soft side too; you just had to know them well before that side of their personality came out. One by one they said to me,

"If Dave's not around for any reason and you need some help, make sure you phone me. Get my number off Dave." They would never give me the number themselves; I always had to get it from Dave. Some sort of respect 'thing' I think. It was very comforting to know that at most pubs or clubs I went to with my mates I had a friend or two on the door! I never took it for granted though, and I think that's why I got on with them all so well. And, of course, no more queuing! But one day knowing these people did come in very handy.

Dave and me were getting on really well. Eventually I took him home to meet my family. Mum and Dad weren't sure about him at first, but after a while, as they saw how he treated me, then they accepted him; you'd think the sun shines out of his arse now! A 'rough diamond,' my Mum calls him. Dave and Mum hit it off right from the start. She doesn't judge people by what they do (not that she really knows what he does) but by how they are as a person. The gentle side of Dave always came out when he was around Mum, and it was really nice to see him relax and talk openly about things to her. If Dave was driving along and he saw Mum walking home from the shops, he would always stop and jump out of the car to give her a big hug. She would get a strange look off his mates in the car and anyone else looking on! Dave didn't give a toss what people thought and never had, and Mum loved it! Dad was not so sure about Dave. It wasn't that he disliked him, but once he knew about Dave's job, he probably knew what he could be like. Maybe that worried Dad a bit because I was seeing him, but they got on OK.

Dave had a rented flat just outside of town, away from the council estate, but just a stone's throw from most of the clubs and pubs, so he was able to walk to work most nights. The first time he took me to his place, I had a pleasant surprise. The carpets were a light creamy colour, so it was shoes off before you stepped through the door. The walls and ceiling were all painted a nice bright creamy colour as well; it was quite big and very tidy for a man, no socks or underpants hanging up anywhere!

A nice looking light brown leather suite with two single chairs and a three seater couch were all arranged facing the usual 'toys' that all single men seem to have! A TV that is too big, but it blends in well with the 'over the top' music system that sits next to it. There were two bedrooms, one was Dave's, painted and carpeted in the same colour as the living room, with a bed big enough for three people! There were no pictures on any of the walls, or any fluffy toys anywhere, which didn't surprise me, just a single photo of his mum and sisters in a lovely wooden frame, sitting on top of his clothes cabinet.

The other bedroom was fitted out like a small gym; nice shiny weights one side with giant mirrors covering most of the wall, and thick black rubber mats instead of carpet, to stop the weights going through the floor boards. On the other side of the room, a great big punch bag was hanging from the ceiling; it looked like it had been beaten to death! The walls behind the bag were covered by lots of really nice photos and drawings of old time boxers doing their stuff in the ring. Some of them had "To Dave, thanks for your help" written across them. I had a little smile at myself in the wall of mirrors, he was so proud of his gym, he looked almost like a child playing with his toys as he showed me how they all worked. But when he had a go at the punch bag I thought the bloody ceiling was going to fall down he hit it so hard, but he finished it off with one of his great big smiles.

The kitchen wasn't very big; you could see where someone had taken down a wall to make it into a sort of kitchen diner, which gave it a bit more space; there was only healthy food in the fridge, which matched the TV and music system in size.

Dave made us both a bit of lunch, and then he took me to the council estate to meet his family, only a short drive away. As I got out of his car I could tell straight away it wasn't the place to be if you didn't live here, and Dave started to act differently as well. It was almost as if he was back at work doing the doors. His body language changed from being slow and relaxed, into sharp, confident movements, and the few people that were hanging around got a piercing glare until they turned and looked the other way. I haven't been on a council estate before, and if I wasn't with Dave I wouldn't have felt very safe. As soon as we were inside his Mum's flat, he went straight back to 'Mr Slow and Relaxed' again. It was a world away from the other side of the front door.

His Mum, Sue, gave me a lovely cuddle; she made me feel so welcome, and soon we were chatting away over a cup of tea, talking about Dave when he was a wee boy in shorts!

" Right!" he said to us, jumping out of his chair. "If you two are going to take the piss, I'm off to sort out some business." He gave me a little kiss, then wrapped his arms around his mum and lifted her off the ground;

"I'm not so little now, Mum!" Dave said with a big smile. Sue told him to put her down or she would put him over her knee and smack his bum, but you could tell she was so proud of her boy. He put her down and gave her a peck on the cheek;

" See you in a bit," he said.

Chapter Three

1968

Dave grew up on a big council estate in south London. When he was a young boy, his father went for a walk one morning and never came back. His Mum wasn't bothered, but Dave was only 10 years old, and he was devastated. It left some deep emotional scars. Dave had a sister, Barbara, who was only eleven months younger than him, and two older sisters; Jade was nearly twelve and Louise a year older, so his Mum had her hands full. He was just like all his mates now and nearly all the other kids on the estate, no Dad, and no discipline.

It was a very violent estate, everything revolved around drink, drugs or turf. Loads of kids fighting over something or nothing, then they would get together and fight the Asians, or 'Pakis' as most people called them. Dave and his mates hated them and they hated Dave and his mates. The more 'Pakis' that moved on to the estate, the more they were hated.

"Let's go Paki bashing tonight!"

"Fucking Pakis, taking over our country!"

"Mister Fucking Paki!"

The little gangs would egg each other on, and the shops on the estate were always an easy target. The kids would smash their windows as often as they could, sometimes even when the shop was open, then terrorise the family.

The council sectioned off a bit of waste ground next to the estate and made it in to a play area to try and help the younger kids, but it soon got vandalised like everything else, and ended up as a fighting arena for the older kids.

Dave's mum tried to make him go to school every day but he just wasn't interested. She was working very long hours trying to make ends meet, so at the end of each day she was too tired to argue with him. Whenever Dave came home with a black eye or blood running from his mouth she could always find that little bit of energy to gently tend to his wounds and cuddle him better, and that's all Dave wanted.

A small boxing club opened up behind one of the pubs on the estate. Dave and a couple of his mates went and had a look through one of the dirty cracked windows. Nothing fancy, not even a proper ring to fight in, just lines painted on the floor in a sort of a square. The punch bag hanging from the rafters that had seen better days, two pairs of old boxing gloves lay on the floor in the middle of the lines, all four gloves were different colours and sizes. They poked their heads around the door for a closer look. The atmosphere was electric, but as soon as Dave and his mates walked in everyone in there looked over to them and stopped talking, it went dead silent. Then one of the old guys slowly walked over to them. He was a big angry looking hard nut, and you could tell he wasn't happy about Dave and his mates being there.

"What do you want?" he said to them.

Dave asked if they could watch. The old guy looked down at them for a bit, then he crossed his arms and started to rub his chin with one of his hands; it was so quiet you could hear his fingers scraping against the stubble!

"OK, but keep your mouths shut and no messing about," he said. He walked back over to the others, and it was almost as if someone had flicked a switch, they were all excited again. The three of them stood in the corner and watched a couple of bouts. The young kids would try and beat the fuck out of each other; there wasn't much skill, just fists, elbows and the odd head butt coming in from all directions. When all the kids had finished, and the blood had been wiped up off the floor, the older boxers had a right old tear up with each other, then shook hands, had a couple of cans of beer together, ready for the same again the next day!

Dave and his two mates started going in there most nights. It turned out that the older fellas were great; they would show them what to do for about half an hour, and then put boys of roughly the same size up against each other. They loved watching the youngsters beating the shit out of each other! They were always made to shake hands after each fight, and if one of the kids didn't want to shake, then he would be told not to come back. That was that; no second chances. A few simple rules and some discipline made everyone get on with each other. It was strange for Dave and his mates to have rules and boundaries to stick to, but it brought some kind of normality to the day. After all the bouts had finished the friendly arguing about who had beaten who began, and then the bets were sorted out.

Sometimes the old guys would start talking about the good old days, trying to outdo each other with what they all got up to. Some used to be bank robbers, some were street fighters, debt collectors and personal minders, even a couple of murderers! Not your out-of-control, high-on-drugs killing anyone, but other villains like themselves. For some reason this was acceptable amongst these people.

The one thing Dave noticed, that stood out more than anything, was that they were always polite to each other. Yes, a lot of swearing and banter;

"You fat old git, about time you kicked the bucket!"

"Huh! I'll see you out, you ugly old bastard!"

But always with a smile, a pat on the back or a handshake, and of course, a little bit of 'pretend' sparring to finish off! When the bar girls from the pub came in with some drinks for the young lads, the swearing would immediately stop. Of course there was a lot of piss taking from the old guys, but nothing too rude, and the girls would give back as good as they got. If any of the young boys used bad language in front of the girls, a slap around the head would soon put them in their place.

Dave loved this dingy back street room. As soon as you walked in it was, "Hello Dave, nice to see you mate!" with handshakes and some 'pretend' sparring as well. They trusted each other in there, everyone stuck to the simple rules without preaching them all the time. Even the betting on the bouts was fair. If the fight was a close one and they couldn't decide who the winner was, they just gave each other's money back.

"I'll get you next time you old fart!" more handshakes, a pat on the shoulder and a smile. The older guys always made a fuss of the young kids. It takes guts to have the crap knocked out of you, and then come back the next night for some more. Although these men were not your ideal model citizens, the boys still looked up to them. Maybe it was just those few rules and a bit of discipline the kids needed. But as soon as everyone walked out of the boxing club through the door and back onto the estate it was different, no one trusted anyone any more, and they all went their separate ways.

Chapter Four

Dave 1972

I was just 14, and decided it was time to leave my school-teachers in peace, not that I was there that often anyway! When I say 'decided,' one day a mate and me were walking home from school; we suddenly turned to each other and said "Bollocks to that!" We both burst out laughing and never went back!

So it was time to find some work. Not in an office, or a shop stacking shelves, that would drive me mad. Even at 14 I was quite big, so I lied about my age and blagged my way onto a shitty old building site labouring for some bricklayers. Not that they cared how old you were. As long as you could do the job you got your money, and it was cash in hand.

Mum didn't mind me working at my age, the longer I was off the streets the less trouble I could get into, and I didn't have to keep asking her for money all the time. I enjoyed the hard graft, but that job didn't last long; they were a right bunch of moaning old farts, and I used to get covered in cement. Then I had a couple of months helping some roofers, they were much more fun, but the work wasn't regular. That's how it went on for about three years, going from job to job, not really knowing what I wanted to do.

The boxing club was the only thing I looked forward to most days. The people living on the council estate just drifted along from day to day, the same sad old faces, they seemed to have got lost in their own little world. I hated the thought of being stuck in that place for the rest of my life.

I was working on a building site for some more grumpy old bricklayers with a good mate of mine, and we started watching a gang of scaffolders doing their stuff. It was summer, so they had their shorts on, and their tops off. They worked hard but were having a good laugh at the same time, and they weren't covered in brick dust and muck. Every now and then they'd have a competition to see who could lift the most tube or who could run up the ladder the quickest; there was plenty of piss taking as well! We spoke to their foreman to see if he had any work for us.

"Start tomorrow if you like," he said, shrugging his shoulders, "give it a go."

We met them in a café the next morning at 7.30, just down the road from the building site they were working on. Even that early in the morning the piss taking had started, all of it aimed at us two 'new boys'! It didn't bother us; we just gave it back as best we could. We both loved it, lifting steel all day was like being down the gym, and we enjoyed all that non-stop piss taking! We even started to take the piss out of the moaning old bricklayers that we'd helped the day before! They tried to give it back but all the other scaffolders joined in and slaughtered them! We just laughed all day, it was great, and the money was a bit better. I always gave Mum half my wages. She had worked very hard to give us almost everything so now it was payback time. My two older sisters were working as well now, so things are getting easier for her at last.

We have always been a close family. If one of us has a problem, we all rally round together to sort it out. If it were a boyfriend then I would sort it out. My sister Jade had been seeing this fella called Allen. She was a good-looking girl who had no trouble getting boyfriends and no one knew what attracted her to him. During one of their many rows he got a bit physical and hurt her. I had never liked him, so it gave me a good excuse to go and hurt him. He was older than me and had a bit of a reputation as a hard man and a bully. I made a couple of phone calls to find out where he was, and went to the little cafe he was eating in.

I walked in, said nothing, tore him to pieces and loved doing it! I had a quick look around the place. I knew a lot of people in there and they knew me through my reputation. Mine had just gone up a notch and his just went down. You could tell no one cared about him, they wouldn't say anything about this. He had it coming; one punter even raised his mug of tea, as if to say 'Cheers for that mate!' then he turned away and carried on drinking it as if nothing had happened! I found out later that Allen had a little protection racket going on the estate, collecting money off the Pakis that owned the shops, so he got another good beating and I took it over.

The scaffolding was going well, I picked it up really quickly, and it wasn't long before I had my own lorry and a gang of men. I didn't have a driving licence, but the boss man didn't care as long as he didn't have to take the lorry out himself and the work got done.

It was good being in charge, it felt natural to be telling people what to do, but we all made sure we had a good laugh as well; it made the day go much faster. I loved scaffolding but after a couple of years, I felt like I needed to do something else.

I didn't go to pubs and clubs that often, I hated all the silly drunks, but it was one of my best mates' birthdays, so a night out was called for. We went on a pub-crawl. Not your normal crawl though; I never drank and the others didn't go over the top either.

We thought we would try this new club called Champs that everyone kept talking about, just out of town. Only ten minutes in a cab, and we were standing with all the other people waiting to get in. It was a long queue but most of them were behaving. All the way along the path they had gold plated metal stands with thick dark red rope going through the top, to separate the punters and the public, and to stop people pushing in the queue. It was a big place and looked very impressive with all the glittering lights out front. As we got closer to the entrance I started watching the doormen, they seemed to be really enjoying themselves! Telling the drunks to piss off politely, as well as the people who tried to push in, and chatting to all these lovely girls.

Then it hit me!

I started to get all excited! This was what I wanted to do. A night out, have a good laugh, talk to loads of girls, throw some Pakis across the pavement and get paid for it! All night I watched the bouncers working, trying to keep the club running smoothly. I even started looking around myself for troublemakers. They were so easy to spot I felt like going and sorting them out myself. This is it; I knew it was for me. It's strange how people don't know what they want to do in life, then they see someone else working and it just hits them; this is what they want to do.

I couldn't get to sleep that night, all I could think about was the door work. It was going over and over in my head, every move the bouncers made, and everything they said, but it was me talking instead of them.

I started to ask about at a couple places, but all I got was; "Sorry mate, without any experience we can't take you on." Maybe it was my age, because it definitely wasn't my size! I was only just nineteen but a big lump!

I decided to take my driving test, just in case I got caught driving, and got banned before I'd even got my bloody licence! The test turned out to be harder than I thought; taking the scaffolding lorry out every day had given me some really bad habits. I could drive well enough, but not like you should do to pass the test. But I passed first time! Maybe it was the bullshit compliments I gave the girl examiner!

I bought an old banger, so we started going to different places a bit further out of town. At first we found it hard to get into some places, we didn't know the doormen, plus we were bigger than most of them! But I was a good talker and we soon got to know most of the bouncers, they knew we weren't trouble.

There was this one particular club we liked, the doormen were quite friendly, not our best buddies but they always said 'Hello' to us. There never seemed to be any trouble inside or outside, and there was always a good atmosphere.

I was still enjoying the scaffolding, working bloody hard, boxing or weight training most nights, and of course plenty of Paki bashing. Still all I could think about was doing the door work. I asked some of the old timers from the boxing club if they could put the word about that I was looking for some door work, but nothing came from that. A couple of weeks later I went to a favourite club with a mate from the boxing club. We never got there early and we always queued up the same as everyone else because we didn't want to take the piss. As soon as the doormen saw us they would wave us to the front,

"Hello lads how are you?" they'd say.

But tonight there was only one and he seemed to ignore us. When we did eventually get to the front there was no 'Hello mate' or friendly handshake, he just gave a nod of his head, and then went back to concentrating on the queue line.

'Fuck him!' I thought to myself. One minute they're shaking our hands, the next they're ignoring us, 'Fuck them!'

As we got further inside we passed the other bouncer who was usually on the front door as well. He looked very agitated;

"Hello lads, how are you?" he said, then ignored us and went straight back to work. Well fuck him as well!

We put our coats behind the counter. There was something different about tonight, all the staff seemed to be on edge for some reason. We made our way over to the bar, and when the girl came over to serve us, even she wasn't herself.

"What's going on tonight?" I said to her.

"Three stag parties have managed to get in, and only half the bouncers have turned up! It's going to get messy later," she said. You could see as the night went on, something was going to happen. If you leave them alone, sometimes it sorts itself out. If you start dragging them out one by one, all hell can break out. And it did, big time!

Two bouncers on the front entrance had to stay there to stop the idiots that had been thrown out from getting back in, which left three bouncers inside. They were going to earn their money tonight! We were standing back watching the drunks trying to punch and kick the fuck out of each other. The bouncers were trying to drag them out one by one. I was getting a sort of buzz, pretending it was me dragging them out! The head bouncer never said anything to anyone. He was about six foot six and just as wide. He wasn't nasty or loud and always looked calm and in control, just getting on with his job. Tonight he was definitely not calm. He was trying to protect the main bar from all these idiots. The girls behind the counter were scared and two of them were crying. I hate drunks; they spoil everyone's fun.

Suddenly I spotted a face I knew. Fuck me! It was Allen, the big bully that hit my sister! He seemed to like seeing the bouncer getting a good kicking. There were about 15 drunks against one bouncer each one running forward to try and get a punch or a kick in. The wankers! He was only doing his job. The more I saw the so-called 'hard man' laughing the more my blood boiled. Fuck it! In I went, not looking at anyone else but the bully, and thinking about my sister. He didn't even have time to stop smiling! I ran at him, hitting him as hard as I could. You could hear his bone break even with all the noise. His jaw went sideward and stayed there. The rest of him hit the floor like a sack of potatoes. It was time to show this doorman what I could do.

Two.... three.... four single punches, another three drunks out of the way. We stood back to back, the bouncer and me, fighting these wankers, and soon the tables turned and it was all over as quickly as it started. After we had thrown the last drunk out the back door with a head butt for good measure, he just looked at me;

"Nice one!" he said, and went straight back to work.

Of course my mate and me didn't have to buy another orange juice for the rest of the night. As we left, the head doorman asked me,

"Are you still looking for some work?"

"Yes, but no one will take me on without any experience."

"Here's my mobile number, if you need a reference, tell them to phone me. I'm Steve. See you later," he said.

The other two doormen gave me a thank you nod; I gave them a nod back, as if to say 'no problem!' they told me again, the boss-man's name was Steve, but I think I will call him Big Steve!

I made a few calls, and tried some clubs and pubs. I gave Big Steve's mobile number as a reference but all I got was silence, then, bluntly; "We'll be in touch."

I didn't hear anything for a couple of weeks, which gave me the hump a bit. I'd helped out big time that night and all I got was some free orange juice and a bloody mobile number!

We were really busy at work so it took my mind off it a bit, then I got a phone call from this girl to come and see her about some door work. 'Great!' I thought. I have never had an interview before; I wondered if it was like going to get a job scaffolding; "You got a job mate, yeah, start tomorrow." Then, if you're no good they just tell you to piss off!

I put on my best jeans polished my shoes and bought myself a nice new shirt to try and look the part. I turned up at the address she gave me, a small building but very smart. No signs outside and the front window had been blacked out so you couldn't see inside, just an intercom button by the side of the door. I pressed the button and the same girl who'd rung me said, "Yes?" in a very unfriendly way.

"It's Dave; I've come about the job."

"Hello Dave, glad you could make it! My name's Kate." Her voice was very friendly now! "Please come in," she said.

I tried to open the door a couple of times, but had to press the intercom button again to speak to Kate.

"Sorry, Dave," she said, and then started on about the bloody electric lock and how it was better when they were on the ground floor and she could just walk over and open the bloody thing herself! She finally managed to unlock the door. I went in and she met me at the top of the stairs. I'd thought she was the secretary, but it turned out she was doing my interview! She was about 35, very slim with a fake tan and long blond hair, but lovely looking, very friendly, and she made me feel at ease straight away. I'd thought there would be some big old lump with a crooked nose, grinding his teeth and growling at me the do's and don'ts! Then they would make me fight someone to see how good I was!

She made me a cup of tea, we just sat and talked for about half an hour about nothing special, and we had a real good laugh. Not one word was mentioned about the job. Like did I have any experience of door work, if I thought I could do the job or not. I thought it was all a bit strange. Then she just said,

"When can you start?"

I said "What, you can tell from a little bit of banter that I've got what it takes to be a doorman?"

"No" she said, "I spoke to Steve and he said you could work with him anytime. Whatever you did that night must have been a bit special, he's not one for paying compliments."

'Nice one!' I thought. Big Steve sacked the bouncers who hadn't turned up that night, and I got the job.

The two doormen I was put with were the same ones I had helped out the night it all kicked off. They turned out to be good guys and we got on really well right from the start. They both shook my hand and thanked me for my help. One said, "Thanks for your help the other night, fella, its great to have a lunatic on board! If you're not sure about anything, ask someone else because we haven't got a clue!" The two of them burst out laughing and couldn't stop! I started to laugh as well, not sure if I was laughing at what he'd said or how much it made them laugh! The one thing I was sure of, I was going to get on great with these two!

It felt a bit strange at first, being on the other side of the queue, but after a couple of hours, just like with the scaffolding, it felt natural to be standing there telling people what to do. I was getting such a buzz out of it. The night went well; not too much trouble, just the odd drunk and queue jumper to sort out.

The more I chatted with the other two doormen, the more I realised we'd all had the same sort of upbringing. No Dad. No discipline. Go and learn how to fight or get bashed up. Try and earn some money where you can, and look after your family. I had a great laugh with them; we let our guards down, and got to know each other really quickly. We swapped mobile numbers at the end of the night, and they both said that if ever I need a hand to give them a call. I said the same to them.

I started doing the door work seven nights a week. Four nights at Big Steve's club and the other three wherever I was needed, so the day job had to go. But I was earning good money and I was doing something I loved, plus I still had the protection money coming in from the Paki shops. This meant I wouldn't smash up their shops and as long as they kept giving me money, no one else would either.

Life was on the up. I had enough money to rent a flat off the estate, but not too far away. I still had to look after my family, and keep an eye on my little protection racket. Every now and then a small gang would form on the estate, or a new family would move in to the area. They would give the Paki shops some agro and try and cash in on my patch. They were sorted out quickly and violently. If you do it by yourself and inflict enough pain without giving a fuck about anyone, it leaves a strong message behind. Mess with me and pay the price.

I always made sure the door work was kept totally separate from my other stuff. They sort of knew what I was up to, but I never spoke to Kate or Big Steve about it and they never really gave a toss.

I was getting on well with the door work and getting a good reputation for sorting things out. Most of the doormen were happy to turn up for work and be told what to do without taking on any responsibility. Some of them had a laugh, and some were grumpy. Fuck the grumpy ones! I loved being the front man ... well, just behind Big Steve!

After about eight months of working and fighting alongside Big Steve, Frank and Pat, it was obvious to me, and everyone else that I was well capable of being in charge. The chance came sooner than I thought. Kate called me into the office one day and said they were getting a bit of trouble at this particular club.

"The owner is a good friend of Steve's, and they give us a lot of work, but he hasn't got the time to go and sort it out himself. Steve trusts you Dave; this is your big chance to prove yourself. You'll be in charge of the door staff. They've all been told. There's enough staff there but it's just not happening."

"OK Kate," I said, "but I'll need Frank and Frank to give me a hand for a couple of nights."

"That's fine," she said, "I'll tell them to meet you there tomorrow."

Frank and Frank were the two doormen that I had met on my first night's work. We have worked together loads of times since then and have stayed good friends. Only one was really called Frank, but Pat decided to call himself Frank one night to confuse the rest of the staff. Every time someone called out 'Frank' the two of them would reply, then one of them would pretend to get the hump because he wasn't needed! They both just giggled all night long with each other! They've done it so often that now most people think that Frank is Pat's real name! Two good guys, not your stupid types. They like a laugh and are always playing jokes on people, like two little kids in giant bodies! When the three of us work together we use up more energy laughing than throwing people out! They never take the piss in a nasty way, just a bit of fun, but when the shit does hit the fan they can be trusted 100 percent.

I turned up early at the club to have a chat with the owner and get a feel for the place. His name was Giles and he wasn't what I'd expected; he was very slim with dark slicked back hair and a very expensive looking suit. He was more your businessman than a nightclub owner, but he seemed OK and made me feel welcome. He showed me to his office and made me a fresh orange juice with some shiny chrome plated contraption that didn't work very well. The amount that came out didn't match the amount of oranges that went in, but it tasted lovely, and I thought to myself that I could do with one of those. I sat down in one of his big leather chairs, and then we talked about the trouble he was getting and where most of it happened. Inside mainly he said, but the bouncers seemed to be throwing out the wrong people. Straight away I knew what the problem was. The doormen were letting in their own friends, and they are not going to throw out their mates. I didn't tell him that I knew; he was nervous enough as it was.

It was a big club, and they started letting people in at 8.30. I asked him what time he briefed the staff.

"I don't," he said. "My head doorman does it for me." Another mistake, I thought to myself.

At 7.30pm on the dot, Frank and Frank showed up, already laughing. Just seeing them makes me smile! Why can't all the boys be like these two? Life would be so easy. They always turn up one hour early; have a coke and chill, probably working out their wind-ups for the night!

One by one the rest of the door staff turned up. I told them to grab a coke or something and meet on the dance floor for a briefing. It's 8.15pm and still only eight out of the thirteen doormen were here. I had seen a couple of them before but the rest were strangers to me, which can be dangerous. If it kicks off and the guys you are with bottle it, you're in trouble. At least I knew Frank and Frank were here. I was explaining who was going to stand where and trying to remember names when the rest of the fellas turned up. I watched the five of them slowly walk downstairs onto the dance floor talking to each other as if we weren't even there. Five minutes before the club opens and they can't be bothered to hurry up. That gave me the hump straight away. They eventually made it over to us.

"Hello chaps," I said, trying to speak in a friendly voice, just in case they were OK. "My name's Dave. As you all know, they've had too much trouble here lately, so I've come to find the problem areas and iron them out. Is there anything you'd like to say about it?"

The one in front said, "No, it's fine mate, we can handle it." That gave me the right fucking hump, even Frank and Frank stopped smiling; they knew what was coming next.

"Let's get one thing straight," I said. "I'm not your fucking mate and you can't fucking handle it."

There was no reply, just dead silence. You could have cut the atmosphere with a knife. Then two of the five walked forward, big fuckers, but out of shape.

"Who the fuck do you think you are coming in here taking over our club?"

I wanted to rip his fucking face off.

"It's not your fucking club," I said to him, "you are here to look after it." Now I'm thinking 'how many of these are friends?' I know Frank and Frank will be thinking the same thing. Three against thirteen! Time to act! I took one step forward and hit the biggest one as hard as I could. Twenty something stone of fat went down like a sack of shit! I moved away from the other big fat fucker quickly, but looked him straight in the eyes to wait for a reaction. I knew the two Franks would already know which ones were going down first. If this goes off now someone is going to be badly hurt. No reaction from anyone. If anything were going to happen it would have gone off straight away. "Drag that fucker out of here," I said to the other one.

He dragged him by one arm across the dance floor to the stairs, then waited a few minutes until he came back to life a bit, and then they struggled up the stairs. The bar staff were watching, open mouthed!

"Right," I said to the others, "if anyone wants to leave, now is a good time."

Frank looked at me and mimed 'you nutter,' then poked out his tongue, I was trying my hardest not to laugh! I organised them the best I could; Frank and Frank inside, thank fuck they were here. I could concentrate on the front of the club.

As soon as everyone was in place and settled down, I made a quick phone call to Kate.

"Sorry Kate, I had to let the head doorman go, can you tell Steve? I'm sorry."

"Listen Dave," she said, "Steve already knows. I don't know what it is with you but as far as Steve's concerned you're in charge now. Steve said fuck them, what's done is done. But he said be careful, they might come back."

The night started off OK, just like any other club, but messy. The rest of the doormen seemed OK, but had been led astray by the two fat ones who were in charge. I tried to break the ice with the three I had on the main entrance, but they were still not sure of me. I went inside now and again to check on the Franks. They were both laughing which meant everything was fine! They didn't see me, but now and then the laughter would stop, they'd have a quick look around the place for trouble, then one would say something to the other and they were off again! I smiled and went back to the front doors. The club was fairly new, and classy, so everyone wanted to try it out. But there were rules. No trainers, no stag parties, and definitely no drunks.

The pubs started to turn out. This is when most of the trouble begins, plus at the back of my mind were the two fat boys. Are they going to make an appearance later? Fuck them if they do, I will hurt them big time.

The queue was long. About fifty people, they were all quite well behaved and just having fun. Then these three fellas walked straight past everyone right to the front of the queue.

"Hello mate!" one of them said to us. I could tell they knew the doormen I was standing with and I could tell they would always get in without queuing. Why was no one telling them to get to the back of the queue? I stepped forward.

"Not tonight lads." They gave me one of those 'Yes I am' looks.

"Go and get Bill," says one of them, "he's a good mate of mine and always lets us in."

Who the fuck does he think he is, talking to me like that; Bill was the sack of shit that had to go earlier.

"Time to go lads, Bill doesn't work here any more," I said.

They hesitated for a bit then, just walked off. I knew that wasn't going to be the last time I saw them. It happened a few times as the night went on, but each time they walked away without an argument.

Something strange was going on. I went inside to see if Frank and Frank were OK. They had separated and their smiles were missing, which meant trouble. I stayed on the higher level so I had a good view of the dance floor. Seven or eight fellas were getting right out of order. As I got closer I thought, 'Fuck, how did that lot get in?' It was the ones that knew Fat Bill. I made my way over to Frank and told him they'd all been turned away, and how the fuck did they get in? We looked at each other... the back door. One of those tossers had let them in through the fire exit. I thought it was strange that none of them had argued with me when I said they couldn't come in tonight.

"OK Frank," I said, "You keep an eye on them; I'm going to find the wanker who let them in."

I'm walking over to the fire exit trying to work out how to get this sorted without the club getting smashed up. It's bad enough sorting out the silly drunks, but sorting out the bouncers as well! Fuck them; I gave the others a chance to leave. No more chances this time. The other three that came with Fat Bill were standing by the fire escape doors with silly smirks on their faces. Two more bouncers were close by. A little nod from one of them told me they were all together.

"I need a word outside with you three." They opened the fire exit doors; "You first," I said. Never show your back to anyone, especially your enemies. As the first one turned to face me, I head butted him as hard as I could on the side of his face, he went sideward, his face tensed with the pain, as his eyebrow split wide open and poured with blood. An uppercut under his chin finished him off. Before they could react, number two was on the floor with his face smashed in. Number three came at me,

I tore into him like a mad man, hitting and biting until he stopped moving. Like I said, inflict lots of pain and they will think twice about coming back. I went back inside and made a quick visit to the washrooms to get their blood off me. The idiots were still jumping about on the dance floor.

"OK Frank, me, you and three other bouncers will get these out. Frank will have to stay on the back door." Within five minutes they were out the front making the pavement look untidy. It wasn't long before they left, licking their wounds. Nothing much, just a little slap for trying to take the piss, they wouldn't be back.

The rest of the night was just like any other club. A few drunks had to be thrown out, girls as well as boys. Frank checked out back now and then to make sure they had gone and no one had died, but all they left behind was a couple of pints of blood! After all the punters had gone, I called the rest of the doormen together.

"Right you all know what happened tonight, if anyone has a problem with it, let's sort it out now."

Frank stood one side of them, the other Frank at the back. No smiles, this had to be sorted out now. I looked at each one of them waiting for a reaction.... nothing.

"OK lads, a new start tomorrow, be here at 8 o'clock on the dot please, or you won't have a job."

Kate called me the next morning,

"Hello Dave, can you come to the office today? Steve needs to talk to you."

"No problem Kate, see you soon." As I made my way there I suddenly thought 'fuck, did I go too far yesterday and bash up some of Steve's mates?' I pressed the intercom button, Kate answered in her normal unfriendly voice.

"Hello Kate, its Dave, how are you?"

"OK, darling," she said, "Steve's upstairs. Come up, I'll make some tea and bring it in to you."

'It can't be that bad then' I thought to myself.

Steve was sat behind his nice shiny antique desk, but still looked bloody tall, "Hello Dave, how are you mate?" he said. "A bit hectic last night then?"

"Sorry, Steve, but you know me, if things have to be sorted out then I like to do it properly. How's the boss man? He sort of hid when it all kicked off!"

"Well he wants you there every night as head doorman. You up for it?"

This is what I wanted.

"Well, let me think..." I said. Steve looked at me and got the hump a bit, and then I smiled, "You know I do Steve."

The 'I want to rip your head off' look disappeared from Steve's face, which meant he was sort of smiling. We worked out the extra money I would get; I shook his massive hand, and then went out to celebrate down the cafe, with a nice cup of tea and a bacon roll!

Frank and Frank stayed with me for one week to make sure the other guys were OK, but it turned out they were all fine and glad to see the back of Fat Bill and his mates. After about four weeks the club was running like clockwork, the bouncers were happy, which made the bar staff relax, which made the punters feel at ease. I always stood at the front doors until most of the punters were in, then I'd go inside and make sure the rest of my staff were doing their job. One of the guys I clicked with straight away was Lenny, six foot ten, a bit like the Franks, always laughing and making jokes. He was to become a close family friend and a godparent to my children, which he would take very seriously. It was amazing how many drunks tried to fight him, but they all lost.

After about a year my reputation gave me the opportunity to look after several more nightclubs, which meant more money. Can't argue with that! There was this one incident on the door, six drunks tried to come in.

"Sorry lads. Not tonight." Things got out of hand. Two knocked out, the others were hospital porters. Well, that's what me and Lenny used to call them! Whenever we worked together and trouble was brewing, we'd try to guess who will be the patients and who will be the porters. If it's Pakis they are always patients. I make sure of that. I should thank those six drunks. If it wasn't for them I wouldn't have met my wife Lynn. After they cleared off, I turned to the girls that were standing behind them to apologise.

Lynn just smiled and said, "That's OK." As soon as I saw her I knew I wanted to be with her.

After dating for about a year we decided to get married. We had a big church wedding with all the trimmings. About a hundred people at the reception on and off. Some of the fellas I worked with could only make it for a while because the pubs and clubs still had to be looked after.

I was smiling to myself all night, looking at the faces of Lynn's relatives watching these hard looking giants come and go all night, or Lynn trying to dance with them! One minute she was straining her neck, trying to look up to their faces, or she had her arms stretched out sideways because they were so bloody wide! All night you could hear "Sorry Lynn!" when a size 12 or 13 stamped on her little foot!

These sort of men were usually only seen on a dance floor with a drunk under each arm and one in their teeth, but for Lynn they would do anything. She was a good talker and listener. These men were only human; they had problems like anyone else, and found her very easy to talk to. Pour their hearts out sometimes, but whatever they talked about was never repeated, not even to me. She gained a lot of respect from some very hard and dangerous men.

We were going to wait a couple of years before trying to have kids. I was 23 and Lynn only 19, yet two months later she was pregnant! The next eight months went so quickly and it wasn't long before she was huge. The tables had turned, now my mates couldn't get their arms around Lynn, all they did was take the piss but she didn't care, she just took the piss back!

Dan was born a healthy 9-pounds. Family life had begun. Being head doorman was great, I had everything under control. It gave me a bit of flexibility so I could sneak off and see Lynn and Dan some evenings. I loved my job, my family was great. What more do I need. How about twin girls? Yep, she fell pregnant straight away! Oh well, it's better than having no kids, now we had to find somewhere bigger to rent. Trying to find a house, working nights, one-year-old baby, wife expecting twins, now that is fucking stressful!

After a couple of weeks of searching, we found a lovely place down the end of a very quiet cul-de-sac, so it all came together in the end. I used to think I was earning good money, but with a house and family it definitely didn't go as far, but we managed.

The months just flew by. Dan was nearly two before I knew it; the girls were growing so fast and they were beautiful. I loved going home after work and seeing them all tucked up in bed, sometimes all three in the same one. I would make myself a cup of tea as always, and then I would sit in the kids' room just watching them sleeping. Sometimes I would stroke the bottom of their feet, to see if one of them would open their eyes and give me a smile, but all I usually got was a look as if to say 'leave me alone!' Or I would work my finger into one of their tiny curled up fists, to see if they would hold onto it for a while, just to help me chill for a bit. But I found myself thinking about the council estate.

A new family had just moved in, and were trying to muscle in on my patch. In the end I put it to the back of my mind and got some well earned sleep.

I was woken about five hours later by three little pink things crawling all over me, but it was lovely, and of course a nice hot cup of tea and a couple of rounds of toast. The pink things rolled about on the bed laughing; even at this early age you could see that Dan loved his little sisters.

Lynn and me had a chat for a while, but all I could think about was the council estate; it hasn't been easy running my little racket. I have had some vicious fights with some so called 'hard men'. No way am I going to give it up. I have a family, and I need the money more than ever now. I never told Lynn about this stuff. As far as she knew it was just a few other things that I looked after.

I had a bit of breakfast then it was down to the estate with my angry head on. This shit hole gives me the fucking hump. Best thing I ever did was getting off this place; it was full of time wasters, junkies and drunks. I only came here once a week now, to get my money off the

Paki shops, slap them about a bit if I had to, scare their kids, keep up the fear in them, and take a walk about so people could see me.

I sometimes visit the two pubs on the estate, not for a drink, I just sit there looking around, put them on edge, no one is sure whether they have over-stepped the mark with me. They know what I'm like and they know what I would do; real fear is the only way to keep my patch. I haven't any friends in this run down shit hole any more. There are a few tossers I do talk to just to get all the info I need to keep things running. All they get back is a bit of respect from the other scumbags because they know me. They call themselves informers. Fucking grasses, that's what they are, but I do need them.

The new manager of the first crap hole pub I went in told me I wasn't welcome in there anymore. Who the fuck does he think he is! I grew up on this estate, no one tells me what I can or can't do. I broke five of his fingers in the till then gave him a quick head butt to stop him screaming. He was lying on the floor out cold.

"If any of you mention my name, I'll break all your fucking fingers!" I told the bar staff, making sure every-body in the pub heard. Then I stood there for a short while looking at their faces. I wouldn't remember all of them, but they wouldn't know who I did or who I didn't. There is an old bird behind the bar, she has worked here for years; she knows what I'm like and she will let them know. Fear is the only way to keep power. I have always done what I said I would do and people on this estate know that. Fuck them if they can't be bothered to better themselves and move out of this hole. Who cares, not me. Nothing was ever said to me again in this pub, or the other crap hole. I still need to find my grasses. Where the fuck are they? Time to find the family that want to take money out of my pocket. That makes me very angry, all they'll do is piss it up the wall or stick it in their arm.

Where is that little tosser? He's late. I hate late. My phone rings, it's my grass.

"Where the fuck are you?" I asked. Just silence then we get cut off. It rings again, "Stop fucking about, where are you?" I asked again. They started to laugh at me down the phone. Someone is going to get hurt big time for that. I'll sort them out later. First I have some money to pick up off my Paki banks. The first couple of pick-ups are no problem. Then in the third, two wide boys are giving my Paki friend a hard time and, for once, he looked almost glad to see me! Both of the boys turned around, they knew who I was; their eyes told me that.

"What the fuck do you want?" I said to them. They were trying so hard not to look scared.

"I've been told to collect some money," one of them said. His body was shaking and his lips were quivering as he tried to get the words out, which told me he was shitting it. One head butt stopped him moving, then two more punches to the face as he was going down. The other stupid fucker just froze. He was so shocked at how quickly I'd made his mate look like a pile of bleeding shit with his face hanging off, he couldn't believe his eyes! Not for long. He got it too, but much worse. I looked at the Paki.

"Where are the rest of them?"

"I don't know. They just turned up," he stuttered.

"If I find out you're lying..."

Then he told me they were coming back with guns if he didn't pay. If they need guns that means they are scared of people who don't use them. That sends me a clear message. Guns to frighten a little Indian bloke and his kids! Wankers! Guns! I don't need fucking guns, but I have got to finish this now. I went and found the other shit bag that knows what's going on. He told me where to find them, the dad and one more son. Fuck me! They are living in my old block! Fun time!

Knock - knock!

"Who the fuck is it?" from other side of the door. I'd found out his name from the other grass.

"Mick it's me." As he opened the door I hit him right in the face with a house brick. He was a big old lump, but went down no problem. One more portion of brick just to make sure. I stood up. Son number three had a sawn off shotgun pointing at my face. This lad was only about sixteen or seventeen. We just looked at each other, me with a smile, him with wide scared eyes; he couldn't hold the gun still he was so fucking scared. I had just wasted his big bad old Dad in two seconds, and without a gun.

"Go on then, you little wanker," I shouted at him. "Do it!" My smile was getting bigger as I walked towards him; his mum was standing just behind him. She knew what was coming next. I beat him to within an inch of his life. She was screaming at me.

"Leave him alone you fucking animal, leave him alone!"

After I had finished I picked up the gun, pointed it right in her face and slowly pulled the trigger until the hammer fired. She gasped for air again and again and then fell backwards onto her arse. Did she know it was a fake? Maybe not, but I did. I don't use guns, but I know a real one from a fake one. It would be a while before she was capable of anything. Fuck her and her family.

I still needed to find the wanker who laughed down the phone at me. I dialled and as the phone connected my end, a mobile on the table rang. Fuck me! They must have nicked the grasses' phone! I didn't hang around; the job was done, now back to my other life. Still it was fun while it lasted! I never heard anything about my day out, other than the family had moved on and the message had got around again, do not fuck with Dave! He's a lunatic! That will do for a few months until the next gang turn up.

Nothing much changed for the next few years; my Mum moved off the estate and bought a lovely little house a couple of miles from us with Chris, a bloke she had been seeing for a while. He was a good guy and worked hard; although he was not someone that I would hang about with too often, we got on well enough. He made Mum very happy and was great with my sisters, which was the main thing.

Then, out of the blue, the bank that Chris was working for gave him the opportunity to go and work in Canada for a year. He could take his family as well, all expenses paid. He was divorced from his wife and didn't have any children by her, so he asked my Mum and my sisters if they would like to go. Chris knew how close we all were so he had already spoken to me about it and asked if I would mind.

At first I was a bit annoyed with him, and he started to get a bit worried in case he had upset me. After a while, when my selfish head came off, I began to realize that all I'd ever wanted from the day my Dad walked out on us, was that Mum would find someone nice who would look after her and my sisters, and make their lives better.

She wasn't one for going out with every Tom Dick and Harry, but of the few men she had seen, Chris was by far the best. I shook hands with him and said it would be a great opportunity for all of them, and it might be the only chance they'd ever get to go somewhere like that. We finished our tea and I showed him to the door, he thanked me again this time with a nice relaxed smile. I looked him straight in the eyes and shook his hand again, only this time I held on to it a little bit tighter so he couldn't let go, and then said to him, "You will take very good care of my family, won't you Chris?" and he knew exactly what I meant.

Three months later their house was rented out, and my older two sisters had rented out their flat as well. They had to pretend that they still lived at home with Mum and Chris; it meant a few white lies on the paper-work, or they would have had to pay their own fares.

As I watched them all go through passport control it made me feel very sad; it felt like I should be going with them, but I tried to put on a happy face.

It wasn't long before the letters started to arrive, with some photos of their home for the next year. It was bloody massive, with two great big snowmobiles parked out the front, all of them sitting on one, posing for the camera. They were all smiling and looked so happy, which made me feel a lot better, but I did miss them.

I still loved doing the doors as if it was my first day. The money was coming in regular, but it seemed to go out just as quick. Dan had started junior school, so we needed to buy him a new uniform and loads of other stuff that the school stipulated, and that I'd always thought they supplied. Lots of different types of books, a PE kit, football boots and other bits and pieces. We were being bloody conned by the system as usual! His school bag was so bloody big and heavy he could hardly carry it, the poor little sod, it looked like he was going away for a week, not just going to school for a day!

He was so excited about the new school, even though it was right next door to the infants, where he had just been for the last two years, and in the same building, but you had to go through a different gate. He probably thought he was getting old! Lynn and me gave him a big kiss and a cuddle, and wished him good luck. He walked in the school gates with a couple of his little friends chatting away, they all looked like they were dragging half of their bedrooms with them! Just before they went in the door he turned around and gave us a quick wave, then disappeared inside. Lynn looked at me and burst into tears as if she thought she was never going to see him again! I gave her a cuddle then we went and had a nice cup of tea.

The people we were renting the house from had decided they were going to emigrate to Australia, so the chance came up for us to buy it. I had been thinking about buying something for a while. The mortgage would be a lot more money than the rent, but we loved the house and the road, so it would be worth it in the end, hopefully. The money was going to be very tight; Dan, Samantha and Charlotte were eating nearly as much as me now, god knows where they put it all, so the food bill was growing as well, but we had all that we needed.

Charlotte and Samantha were now at infant school full time, which Lynn hated; not that she didn't like the school or the teachers, she just missed them so much. Lynn applied for a part time job at the girls' school; she said it was to earn some extra money, but I knew it was so she could be near them. Every time I told her this, she'd insist "No, no, it's for some extra money!" Then she'd give me a little smile and rub her hands together quickly, then give me a big kiss and a cuddle! That would always shut me up!

We worked out where we could cut back on the spending and then sorted out a mortgage, and within eight months we had bought our first property. It felt great owning your own house, but because it had always been rented out, it was very old fashioned and needed lots of work to bring it back to life, and to get it just how we wanted it. But with some long weekends and help from my builder mates, we got there in the end; I even built my own gym in the back garden, it was great to have my own space as well. The next five years or so went by so quickly; the kids were shooting up fast, almost too fast.

My Mum, Chris and my three sisters never came back from Canada, they liked it there so much. I was gutted when I got the phone call to say they were going to stay. Mum said that she misses Dan and the girls so much, but the life out here is what dreams are made of. "Your two older sisters have got fantastic jobs on the ski slopes, and go skiing every day. Your little sister is working in the same bank as Chris and doing really well, they've all made some lovely friends out here."

She said Chris had been promoted. If he came back to England he would lose his job and his promotion, and they didn't think they could ever go back to the life in England. I could tell that they loved it out there by the letters and happy pictures they had sent me. I told her it was OK, and we would visit them as soon as we could.

Dan had now started senior school; it was on the same grounds but in a different building altogether, away from the infant and junior school. So it was another bloody uniform for him, and all the other stuff that goes with it, but he did look the dog's bollocks when he first put it on! Of course, after a couple of weeks of climbing trees and doing what boys do on the way home from school, he'd soon made it look like we had bought it from a second hand shop!

Dan and the girls were doing great at school, they all definitely took after Lynn when it came to the brains of the family; they were like sponges, everything you told them would soak in and they would remember.

I was like a bloody breezeblock at school; everything they tried to teach me just bounced off and hit someone else! The only thing that kept my attention was a little bit of woodwork, and that was because the teacher was great. He wasn't your normal teacher and wouldn't have looked out of place standing next to me on one of my doors. I would never forget his name Mr Chisel, or chisel chin because his jaw was so square, but we would never say it to his face. He always had complete control of the class not with aggression or shouting just his presents was enough to keep us in line, plus he was really helpful and seemed to understand where all our anger came from. Maybe his dad had walked out on him when he was a boy. Mr Chisel had a natural talent with wood and he never said no if anyone needed help with something, and the little bit of woodwork I did learn helped when I was doing up the house.

We were very lucky to have great neighbours; a young professional couple one side, who seemed to work 24 hours a day so we didn't see them that often, but they were nice and quiet and very polite.

The people the other side were an old couple, but full of life, they were always smiling and happy, and they loved the children. I liked Stan and Lily from the very first day I met them. Lynn, me, and the kids would always make time to talk to them both. Stan was of the old school, a real gentleman. It was so nice to have great people living next door. Lynn was happy, the kids were happy, which made me happy, what could go wrong?

Every fucking thing, apparently!

Five o'clock on Sunday morning, a knock at the door. 'Who the fuck is that?' I thought and looked out of the window. There were Old Bill everywhere, too many to count.

"What's the matter?" asked Lynn. "Who is it?"

"Don't worry; I've got to go out for a bit," I replied. I kissed the kids; luckily they were still asleep. Lynn knew the score; she had been there a few times before. I put some clothes on and went downstairs to open the door.

"Hello Dave, are you going to come quietly?"

"No problem," I said. I've known this copper for years. We're not the best of buddies, but we have a bit of respect for each other. I run the doors better than they have ever been run, and he knows how difficult it can be to stay within the law when dealing with drunks. But I have made his job a bit easier around the clubs and pubs, so a bit of leeway is given. The fewer people he has to deal with when he's on duty, the more tea he can drink back at the station, and I'm sure that's all he cares about! Nearly twenty coppers tonight, some new ones, and some familiar ones.

"Am I that bad?"

He gave me a little smile; "No. Some are on a training course!"

Never give the Old Bill too much agro. It's like having a go at the bouncers on a club or pub door; you will always come off worse. If it goes to court it looks much better if you didn't resist arrest. Give it to the doormen and you get a slap.

I always had a chat in the van through the peephole.

"Think you fucked up this time, Dave," the copper said. "They had a portable video camera in town last week, doing some sort of police documentary. You were filmed going a bit too far with one of the punters. Some top brass were there. It's out of my hands mate. Hey! You might even be on TV one day!"

As soon as they got me back to the station, they showed me the film evidence, and then charged me. It didn't look very good on my behalf, but they were so fucking smug about it, the wankers! They had me in court the next morning, and I was lucky enough to get bail; all I had to do was give up my passport. It gave me a bit of time to get things in place, I knew I was going down for this one; it was just a question of how long for.

I haven't been inside for a few years now. It was easier when the kids were younger, a couple of white lies about working away normally swung it, but the kids are older now, they know what's going on and it will be hard for them.

I met Big Steve and Kate the day before I went to court, he was great. "No problem with your job," he said, "just keep your head down, and get out as soon as you can. Don't worry about your mortgage either mate, it's already been taken care of."

That was the biggest thing on my mind, and it made it a bit easier not having to think about it, but now all the other shit in my head took its place. I shook his hand and thanked him, and said goodbye to Kate. I tried to give her one of my big smiles, but it didn't work this time. She gave me a sad look, and said to take care of myself.

I stood in the dock listening to loads of bullshit from the big knobs that were videoing me that night; then they put the tape on and showed the jury what a bad boy I was. Nothing was said about the drunk trying to glass one of the bar girls just before we threw him out. But I must admit when I looked at myself beating the fuck out of that wanker, it did look a bit over the top. Still, bollocks to him, he will be getting another beating sooner than he thinks.

They were going on and on about how they can prevent crime with these cameras, a load more bullshit. I started to go into a little trance, thinking about everything, and how the kids would take it.

A couple of days before I went to court, Lynn and me had sat the three of them down and tried to gently explain to them that I would be going to prison for a while. Of course it didn't matter how they were told, it was going to end in tears anyway, and there were plenty of them. That was hard, but it was even harder walking out of the house knowing that I wouldn't be with my family for a while.

The words "Eighteen months" snapped me back to reality; Fuck! I was expecting six to eight, not eighteen! It was a good job we'd left the kids at home with Lynn's Mum. I had already said goodbye to them; seeing them all cry again would have hurt me too much, and I couldn't let them see the Old Bill take me downstairs to the cell. It was bad enough saying goodbye to Lynn, but she gave me one of her reassuring smiles. She kissed her hand and tried her hardest to blow it to me.

I was gutted as they led me down the steps. I looked over at the coppers; they were all shaking hands as if they had just won some sort of battle, and they didn't even look at me, the smug wankers! One day my life was great and things couldn't be better, the next day ......rock bottom! A couple of months are OK, but 18 months is a long time to be away from work, things can go tits up in that time. People are quick to take advantage of you when you're down. I hated being away from Lynn and my lovely kids.

They took me straight to Wandsworth prison, just a ten-minute drive away. I had been here a few times before, so I knew what to expect. Prison is a bit like the council estate; same old fucking faces doing the same old fucking thing, in and out of the nick all their lives. They probably thought the same about me. Fuck them all, as long as they kept away from me.

I settled in quickly and made sure the screws knew that I wasn't going to give them any grief; it just makes life a bit easier. Some of them have been here for years, and they even remembered my name!

All I could think about was the visits from my lovely family, but when they had left I would get very angry with myself, and anyone near me. I'd go straight to the gym and work out until I was so knackered all I wanted to do was go back to my cell and lie on my bed.

I have made some very good friends while working the doors, and they all let me know not to worry, what goes around comes around. What they meant is, if they took time out, normally 6 to 24 months, their jobs were OK when they came out. If they had a family, they were looked after. You never know when it's going to be your turn to take a holiday!

It seemed to be a bit harder this time around. Not the actual 'being inside,' that's the easy bit; anyone fucks with me I bash them. Leave me alone I leave you alone. Simple. The word soon got around the prison not to fuck with me.

I tried to keep things going as best I could from the prison phone. The protection on the council estate wasn't easy to keep under control, but the hardest thing was being away from my family. Not being there for them if things did go wrong. I know that Lenny would be on the end of his phone for Lynn, so if anything did happen it would get sorted, but ...would it be too late?

Big Steve and Kate came as often as they could. Kate would talk me nearly to death, Steve would just grunt now and then, but him being there meant a lot to me. If Big Steve doesn't want to do something he won't do it.

Eight months went by very slowly and things outside were beginning to fall apart. Threats were OK for a short while, but if you don't back them up they mean nothing.

This was the lowest time of my life so far, or so I thought. As soon as I saw Lynn on her next visit I knew things had just got a whole lot worse. No kids, for a start, and she always had a big smile on her face, but not this time. Then I noticed there were no other inmates either. Fuck this. I don't like this. Three wankers and their dad with guns were no problem, but this was scaring me shitless. We had a quick kiss and a cuddle.

"Sit down Dave," Lynn said. People's eyes always tell a story. I knew this was going to be bad. She just came right out with it, as she knows that's how I like things; cut out the bullshit, just say it.

"Dan is in hospital. He's caught some kind of a virus, which has badly affected his kidneys, and they are giving up on him. Dave, it doesn't look good."

The last time I can remember crying was when Dad walked out and never came back, and I sat by the front door sobbing all night waiting for him to come home. Lynn could see this had knocked me for six. It took all my strength to stop the tears from rolling down my face. She knew I would be hurting badly inside at not being able to hold my son. She slowly slid her hands across the table, and held mine as tight as she could, and told me this was from Dan.

We talked for ages about what was going to happen next; she told me she had already let my Mum know. They gave us an extended visit and the screws even left us alone for a while. Same as with the Old Bill, if you fuck with them, they can make your life hell. Play the game with the screws, they will help you out; they only want an easy life. 'Do what you like to each other, but fuck with us and pay the price.'

They gave me a day pass to visit Dan in hospital. He was so ill he didn't even know I was there. I felt so vulnerable, almost naked. I'd always been able to sort things out my way, and on my own, but this was not my world.

We spoke to the doctor in a small cold room. He seemed to know that I didn't want any bullshit.

"His kidneys have almost completely failed," he said. "He needs a transplant. It's the only way to save his life...."

He kept talking, but I had stopped listening after he'd said, "...save his life."

All the good times Dan and me had spent together started to flash in front of my eyes, it was like there wasn't going to be any more. Then the times I had let him down for one reason or another started to come back to me. It almost felt that someone was telling me to never let your kids down.

"Dave, do you understand? Dave? DAVE!" I came back to the cold little room, with Lynn tugging at my arm.

"Yes! Yes, thanks doc," I said to him.

The screws that escorted me to the hospital let me have a cup of tea and some lunch with Lynn, and, of course, gallons of tea for them. After all, it gave them a bit of a break from being stuck inside the prison, plus they were surrounded by lots of lovely nurses, who seemed to be attracted to their uniforms.

The walk from the hospital exit to the prison van was one of the most frightening walks I have ever had to do. I couldn't help thinking that if I made it, would I ever see my son alive again? I tried to walk as slowly as possible; it was like going to school for the first time as a little boy, hands in your baggy grey shorts, head down hoping none of the bullies would see you, and bash you up just for being there.

I sat in my cell with my head in my hands. No wife, no kids, no mates. I was trying to hold it together, but all I did was get angry with myself again for not being able to be there for my family. This is going to be the hardest thing in my life to get through so far ... if I can. Harder than any fight. Even after smashing people's faces in, I can go home and sleep like a baby, no problem.

After a couple of restless nights, and two days of walking around my cell, I took control of myself the only way I knew how. I was in the gym every day, lifting weights for four hours, then on the punch bag for half an hour. After about three months I was in tiptop condition, physically and mentally. But soon this wasn't enough to take away the pain, so I started to take it out on other inmates. It wasn't long before I was back in court on an assault charge. They gave me another three months on top of what I already had left to serve! 'What a prick!' I said to myself. On her next visit, Lynn sat me down and said,

"Dave. Please, please stay out of trouble and come home soon. We need you. Dan needs you."

Then she gave me a picture of him on a kidney dialysis machine, having his treatment. He had tubes everywhere and he looked so thin.

'That's it, no more fights;' I said to myself, 'I have got to get out of here.' For the next few months I trained and trained so hard that I didn't have the energy to fight anyone. All I wanted to do was lie in my cell and get the strength back for the next workout. I was growing faster than ever. Perfect for training when you are in prison, once you have done your bit in the gym, you can just lie on your bed and grow. Because I left the screws alone and gave them a bit of respect, there was plenty of extra food around as well.

The boys were looking after the doors as best they could, also my family. The scumbags were collecting my money off the shit hole for me. Memories of my last visit should linger a little bit longer, until I get out.

Things were not looking good for Dan; he desperately needed a donor. From day one I told them to take one of my kidneys but our blood type wasn't the same. Lynn said the same, but her blood wasn't right either. The only way I can help him now is to stay out of trouble and get home.

Then, out of the blue came the news we had been waiting and longing for! A kidney donor! The match was perfect! And he was a living donor, which was very rare. What a hero!

I had two months left of the first sentence, plus three for the assault. Fuck!

Would I miss the operation?

Would he survive it?

Would I ever see Dan alive again?

All this sent shivers down my spine. Once again the screws saw me right. They put me down for compassionate leave and gave me a really good report. (They weren't really lying; I have stayed out of trouble most of the time.) It came through straight away; only one more week with all these fucking losers. It had been the toughest time of my life so far, and I'd got through it the only way I knew how.

My now massive frame is starting to cramp up in this place. My strength and fitness have helped me on the inside, but will it be enough on the outside?

The sun was shining through the window; I rolled off my bed to my feet and looked out. As I slowly swayed from side to side the sun's rays caught my eyes, past the iron bars,

LYNN

Suddenly came a scream so loud it jolted me from my daydreams of Dave and made me jump to my feet spilling hot tea everywhere! However, what I saw soon made me forget the scalding pain. A bunch of kids were looking over the side of the boat. I froze, unable to move for a second.

"Oh my God, no!" I shouted. I threw the cup away, and ran as fast as possible towards them, fearing the worst. I pushed and shoved the bunch of children out of the way. It was a teacher's nightmare!

Little Steve had climbed over the side of the boat, standing on a ledge hanging on to some rope by his fingertips! Playing dare, probably to impress the girls. With one hand around his arm and the other grabbing a handful of his long blonde hair, I managed to drag him back over the rail.

"My God, what were you thinking, you stupid boy?"

He gazed at me with his beautiful big blue eyes.

"Sorry miss!"

Then he gave me one of his cheeky smiles. I stared at him in anger. Not only for the crazy stunt he's just pulled, (ruining my daydream) but, as usual, he charms his way out of it and I end up being suckered by a 12-year-old again! All the other kids just carried on enjoying themselves, as if nothing's happened, and my little bit of peace has just been thrown overboard with my tea! I grab him by his collar and made him sit with me until we reach France.

We gave all the kids a talking to before we left England. No drinks. No cigarettes (they were much too young for them anyway) and definitely NO fireworks! Some of the boys had started smirking, and I knew what they were thinking. When we said 'no drinking' we didn't mean the teachers as well! We all had a couple, no harm done and all the teachers had a good time.

Then it was back on the coach, a short drive to the boat, and then home to England. It turned out to be a nice, trouble free day until we got to the port and the police were waiting for us. They had been informed that underage English children had been buying up all the fireworks at an open street market! With our bit of broken French, we told the police we had already searched the children and found nothing. There were two women police officers especially to search the girls, and they wouldn't let the coach onto the ferry without a full search, so we had no choice. They knew where to look. Inside their hoods! (Oops! We should have found those!) They'd stuck them with tape to the inside of their T-shirts, and even put them in their bloody sandwiches! A couple of days later we all had a laugh over that one. The police let us go, with lots of head shaking and tutting. Plus a letter was sent to the school to complain about our incompetence as teachers and carers! Apparently, some young children from another school trip had been playing with fireworks a few weeks earlier at the port and they got badly burnt. Not very good publicity. They were just cracking down and trying to blame everyone else.

There was more to come. Big winds mean big waves. They were big, very big, and nearly everyone got seasick. It was a mess all over; sick, sick and more sick! Every toilet had someone's head down it, and the washbasins were over flowing with sick! All the little hard nuts were lying on the floor crying for their Mums, covered in sick! Not a pretty sight. It was terrible, because the other teachers were ill as well and it was left to me, and a couple of older children who came as helpers, to try and look after the rest of them, clean them up and keep them as safe as we could. It was a complete nightmare. Never again! I just wanted to get home to Samantha and Charlotte and find out how Dan was doing.

I'd been thinking about not going on the trip at all, but Mum said I could do with a day out and as the school was paying for all the teachers to go, it wouldn't cost anything. She told me that she would have the girls after school, and that the nurses at the hospital are great, they will take good care of Dan, try not to worry, she said. Try not to worry! Now I am worrying about Dan, the girls, half the bloody school and their teachers! No more bloody boat trips for me!

Finally I got home, and put all my dried, sick covered clothes into the washing machine, and then had one of the longest, hottest showers I have ever had. The smell of all that sick seemed to cling to me. I had a quick cup of tea at Mum's then up the hospital with the girls to visit Dan.

He was looking very poorly today. I reminded him that his Dad was coming home next week, which bought a little smile to his face, and the girls, too. I had a talk with the nurses about the donor; they said everything was fine and the operations should go ahead in two weeks time. I asked them if it was possible to wish the donor 'good luck' by letter beforehand, but they said it really wasn't a good idea. There is a possibility of saying something that may upset them and that could cause all sorts of problems. It's such an emotional time and you don't want them changing their mind, it's better to wait for any contact until after the surgery, if then. They were very sorry, they said, but that's the way it must be.

The week really dragged on, and I spent most of my time up at the hospital. Dan was getting very weak now, the donor had come forward just in time. We'd been so lucky.

At last! Saturday morning, time to go and get Dave! My Mum and Dad were looking after the girls again; I didn't want them to see him come out of prison.

Off I went with Lenny, one of Dave's best mates. He was the first of Dave's mates that I had met. A lovely man, (or a lovely giant!) of about six foot ten with a shoe size to match! Uncle Lenny, Dan calls him; the girls call him Uncle 'Long' Lenny. Not recommended if you don't know him very well! The name came about one morning round our house. Lenny had rowed with his girlfriend and stayed the night on our couch. The next morning Samantha and Charlotte came downstairs, saw Lenny's feet and ankles sticking out of the duvet and hanging over the armrest, and said, "Isn't he long Mummy!" We all had a good laugh, only a couple of six-year-old girls could get away with that! Lenny had a great big smile on his face; he knew that was going to be his name from now on. Uncle 'Long' Lenny! He was great with the kids in his own way, and a very good friend. As soon as Dave was led away, he had turned to me and said,

"Any time, day or night. If you need help, just phone me."

I have only ever rung him once for help. Most of the time I would sort things out myself when Dave was not around, but this time I needed a different type of help.

These yobs started to hang around outside the house on their motorbikes. Normally it was very quiet; everyone made an effort and got on really well in our little cul-de-sac. At first we had no problems from these boys, then they began pushing it, probably to see if anyone was going to challenge them. Little did they know!

A few weeks passed and things had started to happen. Small things at first, cars getting damaged, garden sheds broken into, then a few houses. I came home late one afternoon from shopping and the Dad of these boys had our 68-year-old neighbour, Stan, by the throat! His wife, Lily was beside them both trying to calm things down, but you could see that she was petrified. Stan told me later that the boys had been trying to nick his car. He told them to go away or he would call the police.

"You call the police, I'll make the rest or your life a fucking misery!" the Dad of these boys kept saying to Stan. He turned his head and gave me a very nasty smile.

"What are you looking at darlin'?" he sneered.

Stan and Lily were a fantastic couple; they didn't have a bad bone in their bodies, they loved our kids, and would always babysit the girls if I needed to rush up the hospital to see Dan. Dave thought the world of them, he would do anything for Stan. If he could see this happening... well, it would never have got this far in the first place. Dave has always made sure he gets on with people where we live. If they are nice to him, he is nice back, but Stan was special to Dave. I think he thought of Stan as the Dad he never had.

I dropped my shopping bags and told Charlotte and Samantha to go inside the house out of the way. I told the dad to leave Stan alone.

"What do you think you're doing?" I shouted at him, "he's half your age, take your hands off him!"

"Fuck off, bitch!" he shouted back at me.

"What the fuck has it got to do with you?" His boys started to laugh.

"Just go," I said to him. He let go of Stan's shirt, and said to me, "I'll Be back for you later, you slag!"

He walked off down the road with his arms around his sons' shoulders. His whole attitude said 'you do what you like boys, I'll always get you out of trouble!' It made me so angry!

I took Stan and Lily into our house and made them both a cup of tea. The pair of them was shaking with fear. Poor Stan, even once he was sitting down his legs were still twitching. He pressed his hands on his knees to stop them moving, but then his arms started to shake with them! Lily sat scrunched in her seat trying to drink her tea with her shaking arms. I sat down beside Stan, and gently took his face in my hands.

"This can't go on anymore," I said firmly. "I have to make a phone call."

He picked up his cup of tea by the handle then wrapped his other hand around it, and took a couple of sips, but he kept his head down, as if he was trying to work something out.

Stan is not a silly man, he's seen Dave's mates come and go, he knows what might happen. After a little thinking, he lifted his head slowly, and looked at me with very sad eyes. You could tell that he can guess what will happen, and it will be on his conscience, but he agrees it is probably the only way to get this sorted out.

I gave Lenny a call and explained what had been going on over the last few months, and of course, what had happened to Stan and Lily. He took a very sharp deep breath, and waited a minute before he answered.

"Why didn't you phone me when it first started? I'm on my way!"

I could tell he was very angry with me, but in a good way. Stan took Lily home, settled her in her favourite chair then came back round. Twenty minutes later and Lenny was at our door with two other very handy looking men whom I knew as the two Franks.

"Get the kettle on love," Lenny said, and then bent down to gave me a big kiss and a cuddle. Samantha and Charlotte stuck their heads around the door,

"Hello girls!" They ran straight into his chest and nearly disappeared when he wrapped his massive arms around them! Even at their age he could still throw them around; Frank and Frank just stood at the back of the room, watching. They looked like they have just seen another side to Lenny, and then they sat down for a cup of tea. Stan couldn't believe this big fella could be so gentle, he had only seen them come and go. They never said anything to him, but he always got a reassuring nod. After about 10 minutes of playing a human swing between his legs with the girls, Lenny came and sat down with Stan and me on the couch to drink his tea before it got too cold.

"You must be Stan. Are you OK?" Lenny asked, shaking Stan's hand.

"Yes thanks," Stan answered very quietly. I knew what Stan was thinking; these boys look like they can do some serious damage to someone, and he thinks it will be his fault. Lenny told Stan that Dave talks about him all the time, and he thinks the world of you and Lily. Dave also said that if they need any help, in any way while he's inside it must be sorted out. It brought tears to Stan's eyes, and mine. I pulled Lenny to one side, and asked him not to tell Dave.

"He has more than enough to worry about, this will take him over the edge," I explained.

"No problem," he said, and went back to playing with the girls as if nothing was going to happen. Frank and Frank sat around the dinner table drinking mugs of tea and eating all my biscuits like they haven't seen a biscuit for years, as they always do when they come round here! And you could tell they have never seen Lenny playing with kids before, but they just shrugged their shoulders, the biscuits were much more important!

Stan and me sat down with the Franks for a while to try and have a chat. Like all of Dave and Lenny's mates they were really nice and polite, and tried to make Stan feel at ease with them, but you just couldn't talk to these two properly! All they did was mess around, tell each other jokes and take the piss! They even started to bicker over the biscuits; it was like watching Samantha and Charlotte at the table! Still, at least it brought a little smile back to Stan's face.

At about 9 o'clock there was some noise outside. The boys were back on their motorbikes, with some mates, right outside Stan's house, revving up their engines.

"Time to go to work, girls!" Lenny said and they gave him a big cuddle. Frank and Frank stood up, both trying to grab the last chocolate biscuit at the same time, pushing each other like school kids and they still had the giggles! Lenny gave me a kiss on the cheek, then he looked at Stan and said,

"Don't worry mate, they won't be back." Then shook his hand again. That made Stan even more worried, but he thanked them all for getting here so quickly. Frank and Frank gave me a kiss, shook Stan's hand, then put their thumbs in their ears, wiggled their fingers and poked out their tongues at Charlotte and Samantha! The girls did the same back and wiggled their bums from side to side, so of course the two Frank's did exactly the same back! Lenny and Stan looked at each other, both smiling and nodding their heads as if to say 'can you believe these two!'

The three of them walked to the front door, Lenny opened it, ducked his head and shoulders down and went out first. As the two Franks walked out they both went straight into work mode. Even when they are messing about they look as hard as nails, but when their serious heads go on they look bloody menacing.

As soon as the boys saw these three very hard looking men walk out, their engines revved up again, only this time it was to get away. The three of them got into Lenny's car. Lenny gave me a quick wink and a smile and then mimed 'don't worry,' and then slowly drove after them...

Those boys, or their Dad, never came up our road again. Someone told me a couple of days later it had been very messy, and the family moved away shortly after. Lenny told Dave all about it eventually. Well, he would have found out anyway, but Lenny just played it down a bit.

I was in town a few weeks later with Charlotte and Samantha, just doing some shopping, and a bunch of boys on motorbikes were parked up, five or six of them. They looked at me, then looked at each other, then looked at me again. As I got closer they stopped talking but carried on looking, not staring, just a sort of a 'Do I know you?' look. Were they the boys from that night? I didn't recognise them, they all look the same to me! Not a sound as we walked past. I gave them a half smile. No reaction from them, dead silence. Was it them? Maybe. It was one time I felt really good about Dave and his friends' reputation.

We got home from shopping quite late, the girls had a quick snack and I put them to bed for an early night. I put the kettle on for a cuppa and just sat there thinking of Dave coming home tomorrow, and dragging him straight up the hospital to see Dan. After about ten minutes I heard Samantha and Charlotte creeping slowly back down the stairs. I told them to come and have a cuddle and asked them if they were OK. They were fine, just excited about their Daddy coming home.

The traffic was really bad this morning, probably because of the heavy rain. Lenny was a very good driver; he never rushed anywhere and was always courteous to other drivers, but he did get some funny looks at times. He had to have his seat as far back as it would go, so it looked like he was driving the car from the back seats, and you could only see the bottom half of his head! It felt like I was talking to myself sometimes, he was so far behind me!

I started watching all the other drivers pulling their hair out trying to get to work on time, or wherever it was they were all rushing to. There were all the mums walking quickly along the pavement with their umbrellas bending in the wind, their kids on tow behind them, trying to get to school before the bell goes. I started wondering what their lives were like.......

Were all their children healthy and happy?

Did they all have a husband, a wife, or a partner?

Were they still in love with each other?

Were they all zooming about trying to get up the hospital because one of their children was dying?

We dodged our way through the rush hour traffic; luckily we were going the opposite way to most of it. We got there in the end, with about 15 minutes to spare and parked the car at the pickup point just in front of the prison entrance. Lenny and me have been here a few times before to pick up Dave, so it was nothing new. Lenny knew that I didn't really want to talk, so he tried telling me some jokes to make the time pass quicker. I was only laughing at them because they were so bloody bad, but it worked for a bit. After Lenny had run out of his terrible jokes, we both just sat there, looking at the H.M.P. written across the huge doors in great big letters, now disfigured by the pouring rain that was running down the windscreen. Dave was 20 minutes late coming out and I started to get very fidgety. Lenny turned the radio on and pushed in a rock and roll tape, and then told me not to worry, he'll be out soon. After a couple of songs, 'Jailhouse Rock' started playing. Well! We just looked at each other and burst out laughing!

"Let's have a singsong!" said Lenny, and he started to go for it big time, waving his massive hands in the air from side to side. His singing was even worse than his jokes, but I sang along with him and tried to keep my hands in time with his. The car starting rocking from side to side with us, which made us laugh even more; if anyone had been watching, we must have looked really stupid, but we didn't care! Just as Elvis had finished swaying his hips, a small door opened in the bottom left hand corner of the big doors and I could just make out two men talking to each other. They shook hands, and then out walked Dave with a great big smile on his face. I jumped out of the car. 'Sod the rain!' I said to myself, as I ran up to him and threw my arms around him.

"Christ! What have you been eating?" I said. He picked me up, gave me a great big kiss and we both got in the car.

"Only porridge," he said, and shut the door, his smile even bigger now. Lenny just shook Dave's hand and said,

"About bloody time, mate!" Lenny drove us back, only this time we were going with the rush hour traffic so it took ages to get back home. Lenny knew as soon as he dropped us off that Dave and me were going straight up the hospital to sort out Dan's operation. Lenny is not one for all the doom and gloom stuff, so he tried to cheer us up with some more impressions of Elvis, we had a good laugh, and, for a short while, it took our minds off what was going to happen in the next couple of days.

We pulled up at our house and as Dave got out of the car, Lenny patted him on the shoulder, saying;

"It's good to have you back mate, I'll phone you later." They looked at each other for a bit without saying anything, but Dave knew what Lenny was trying to say, they nodded to each other. It was awful; we knew Lenny loved Dan as much as we did, and I started to cry as the thought of what was going to happen to Dan suddenly rushed back to me. Lenny gave me a wink and then he went on his way. Dave put his arm around me as we walked down the garden path; it felt so good to have him back home. Dave had a quick shower and change of clothes before we went round to my Mum and Dad's house to pick up the girls, then up to the hospital.

As we were leaving the house Stan came out, as always he was dressed very smartly with his tie a perfect knot and his shoes shining. He shook Dave's hand over the little wooden fence that separates our paths.

"It's nice to see you Dave," Stan said, "and thanks for your help."

"No problem Stan," said Dave, "it was Lynn that got it sorted out." Stan looked at me for a few seconds, and then had a little chuckle to himself, turned around and walked back down his garden path towards his house, one hand waving in the air, thanking us again. Dave was so pleased that he could do something for Stan and Lily; they had been a great help, especially over the last year, and have never asked for anything in return.

We drove up to my Mum and Dad's house. Samantha and Charlotte were waiting outside. They ran into their dad's arms as fast as they could; he picked them both up at the same time and gave them a great big cuddle, and lots of kisses. It was lovely to see them back together again, and, of course, Mum got a great big cuddle too! My Dad shook Dave's hand and welcomed him home, but you could tell he wasn't really impressed that his daughter's husband had been in prison again for beating the shit out of someone!

Dave had only seen pictures of Dan for the last few months. He had been too ill to leave hospital and visit his Dad in prison, and Dave couldn't wait to see his son again. We had been rushing around for the last three hours, trying to get up to the hospital as quickly as we could. Finally, when we did make it, we couldn't find a bloody parking space, and we drove around the hospital car park for what seemed like hours, following all the other cars doing the same. At last someone moved out of a space, we parked up and got a ticket out of the pay and display machine for the rest of the day.

We walked in the hospital entrance and up the stairs to the first floor. My Mum, Samantha and Charlotte walked on ahead. We've all been up here so often that we now know all the nurses. As we got closer to the ward Dan was in. Dave seemed to slow down. Then he started to squeeze my hand harder and harder with every step he took, slowing down even more as if he didn't want to ever get there. My hand was starting to hurt, so I had to stop him to ask if he was OK. He had a look on his face that I have never seen before, but I think he was just scared at what he was going to see. He gently cupped my face with both his hands and gave me a big kiss.

"Thank Christ I have got you with me," he whispered into my ear, then he took a deep breath, "I'll be OK, let's go."

The moment he saw Dan I could see Dave was worried, but he put on a brave face, and gave Dan such a big cuddle that his face lit up. He looked so happy to see his Dad, and tried to cuddle him back, but was too weak to keep his arms up for very long. They talked non-stop for about 15 minutes, it was great to see the whole family back together again, but it didn't last long. The nurse came in and told us that the surgeon was ready to talk to us about the operation.

Mum stayed with Charlotte and Samantha, as Dave and me were shown to a small private room. It was nothing special; four blue plastic chairs and a table in the middle of the room, some tea-making stuff, a couple of boxes of old toys in the corner for any young children that might be stuck in here, and a big white clock on the wall. I put the kettle on and made us both a cup of tea, and then we sat holding hands talking about the girls and how they were getting on at school. Anything to try and take our minds off what was about to happen next. We hadn't finished our tea when there was a knock on the door and before we could say anything the surgeon came in.

He was about 50 years old, very short and fat, with not much grey hair, and wearing a long white gown that needed a bloody good iron. He had a folder bulging with papers under his arm. It had Dan's name on the side, which made my heart miss a beat. We both stood up at the same time and faced him. He wasn't what Dave expected, you could tell by the surprised look on his face. The surgeon shook our hands, then got straight on with it. He tried to explain the best way he could, that it wasn't a straightforward procedure, and that a lot of things could go wrong. He said we must understand there was a chance Dan might not even make it through the operation, and even if the transplant was successful, complications after surgery could be a major problem in his recovery.

He didn't stutter, pause or slow down, just carried on talking until everything he had to say was said. He must have done this many times before but that didn't help us, and I wasn't sure how Dave was going to take all this. He has just come home, he hasn't seen or touched Dan for a long time, and is now being told he might die.

There was no reaction from him. Dave had put his arm around my waist to try and comfort me, but I knew he needed it more than I did, so I pulled his arm down to my side, and wrapped both of my hands around his; still no reaction. He was trying to take it all in just as I was. The surgeon started to look a little uneasy. He knew Dave had just come out of prison, and this was the first time the surgeon had met him. Maybe there was usually lots of crying at this point, but Dave just stood there, expressionless. It was all a bit surreal, like a play on the stage. I would say my lines, and now it's your turn, but Dave had forgotten his lines for a moment. He suddenly came back from wherever he had been.

"OK, what's next then?" he asked.

The surgeon cleared his throat.

"There is a lot of paperwork to sort out and sign. Mainly to protect the donor, and us, from any reprisals if things do go wrong. I am sorry; this is common practice in all hospitals. We must sort everything out as soon as possible. Your son is deteriorating by the day and if he gets too weak we won't be able to operate at all. I am sorry to rush you, but time isn't on our side."

We had a quick look at all the forms, we didn't really know what they all meant but we signed them anyway. As the surgeon walked out, another white coat walked in before the door even had time to close, carrying loads more paperwork. It was Zoë, the transplant coordinator that I had been dealing with while Dave was in prison. A really lovely girl, she seemed too young for what she had to do, but was very good at her job. Zoë went through it all again in more detail. She explained it slowly and a lot more gently and carefully than the surgeon had. She also told us that he's not very good at the family thing, but he is one of the best surgeons in the country to do this operation. She said Dan was in very good hands, we must try not to worry, and then left us with a load more forms to read and sign. We tried to read them as best we could and, as with all the others, they were just covering all their backs, so we just put our signatures on all of the forms. Right at the bottom of the last page it said the operation would go ahead in 48 hours. I looked at Dave and gave him a little reassuring smile as best I could and he tried to do the same back.

Zoë came back after about 15 minutes, and made sure we had signed all the forms in all the right places, then told us that all of the paperwork was out of the way. She sat us both down and made sure we knew what was going to happen and in what order. Once she was satisfied that we understood everything, she told us to go and see Dan. We stayed with Dan in his room the whole time, only popping out now and then to go to the loo, or to breathe some fresh air. Then, suddenly, it hit us... The next two days and nights might be all we had left with our son.

Dan knew what was going on. We had to be brave for him as well as each other. Because he had his own room, the nurses let us stay well past the normal visiting times. It got to about 9o/c and we were all getting very tired, Dan needed to go to sleep. Charlotte and Samantha covered him with kisses; Dave and me gave him lots more, and then we made our way home, picking up some fish and chips for our dinner.

The girls went out like a light, but although Dave and me were exhausted we just couldn't get to sleep. We talked into the early hours, and then the pair of us slowly drifted off, but the alarm clock didn't let us lie in. Samantha and Charlotte made some breakfast, and the four of us sat down together. I asked the school if the girls could have the next week off, and they were fine about it, and were surprised that I had even asked!

We dropped them off at my Mum and Dad's house, as it wasn't fair to keep them up at the hospital all day again.

Dan was in a good mood today, as he was feeling a little bit better than he had yesterday. Dave never left Dan's side. They just talked and talked, trying to make up for lost time. Dan kept falling asleep but as soon as he woke up they just carried on from where they left off. The nurses wouldn't let us stay on late today, which was probably for the best.

Zoë took Dave and me back into the little room, and went through the whole of Dan's operation procedure again, just to make sure that we both understood exactly what was going to happen and when. After Zoë had finished we went back into Dan's room and gave him lots more kisses, he told us not to worry and that he would see us in the morning, then he gave us a beautiful smile!

It was heartbreaking... Our brave boy! I held my tears in just long enough to get out of his room so he didn't see me get upset, but as the door closed the tears came flooding down my face. Dave put his arms around me and held me tight until I got myself under control. Thank God he was home with us now.

We drove round to my Mum and Dad's house to pick up the girls and have a bit of dinner; then we went back home for an early night. Dave tucked the girls into bed while I put the kettle on and made us some tea. Lenny phoned to ask if we were OK, his way of saying good luck, and as the evening went on, lots more people rang up to wish us luck.

We didn't go to bed very late, and somehow Dave and me both managed to get to sleep straight away. We were up and out of bed by 7 o'clock, which gave us plenty of time. A quick shower, as the girls did their stuff with the breakfast again, then in the car and up to the hospital.

As soon as we walked into his room Dan gave us such a great big smile, he was so glad that the time had come at last. Dave sat with him while I went to find Zoë and make sure everything was OK, and there were no problems. The doctors and nurses were in and out of Dan's room all morning, checking him for any reactions to all the new drugs they had to give him before the operation.

My Mum and Dad came up to see Dan, and to take Charlotte and Samantha for walks around the grounds of the hospital, trying to take their poor little minds off what was going on. Just as they came back from one of their walks, a nurse popped her head around the door and told us it was time to take Dan very soon. We both gave Dan some big kisses and cuddles. The girls did the same, and then they stuck a picture onto the headboard of his bed that they'd drawn of the whole family together on a beach. It had the words:

'LOOK EVERYONE! OUR BROTHER HAS A NEW KIDNEY!'

Now the tears started to flow, even Dave. The doors opened again, two nurses and a porter walked in.

"Are you ready? We must take him down now."

"Yes, the nurse came in five minutes ago and said you would be here soon," I replied.

They were all so kind to us. Dave and Samantha were on one side holding Dan's hand; Charlotte and me were on the other side holding his other hand, none of us would let go until we got to the operating theatre.

One last kiss and then they all went through the doors. As they were closing we caught a glimpse of the donor already in position, with lots of people around him, in their green outfits, white masks and hats, and with silly looking plastic shoes on as well. That reminded us that we should be thinking of the donor and his family as well. We stood outside the theatre with the girls for ages, all with our arms around each other; not saying a word, just wishing that all this would go away. A nurse came over and said, "You would be a lot better off back in the room. Try and get some rest if you can." Mum and Dad took the girls back to their house for the rest of the day.

Dave and me sat next to each other, holding hands, not knowing what to say to each other. We just sat there. Every now and then someone would come in and ask if we needed anything.

"No thanks. Any news on Dan?" one of us would ask; they gave us the same answer every time;

"The surgeon will let you know as soon as he can." They told us it should only take about three hours, if things go OK.

The big white clock seemed to tick louder and louder as time went on, every hour seemed like a whole day, why do they put them bloody things in here?

I made another cup of tea for us both, then we started talking about the great times we've had with the kids, the places we have taken them. We started trying to reassure each other that it was all going to be OK and plan where we are going to take Dan and the girls as soon as Dan can leave hospital. More silence for a while, then suddenly Dave jumped up out of his chair, and put both hands in the air, as if he was talking to the world;

"The beach!" he cried, "That's it! Yes! A family day to the beach, with Dan's new kidney! Let's celebrate with a dance!"

He held out his hand to me; I took his hand and stood up, then we cuddled into each other and slowly started moving to the imaginary music that was in our heads. After a couple of minutes I asked Dave which song he was dancing to, he stepped back a bit and tried to swivel his hips.

"The same as you," he said with a smile. I knew it was the record we had danced to on our first date, and he couldn't dance then either, but he was right.

"Which beach would you like to go to?" Dave asked me. I moved in close to him again and held onto him really tight, thinking how nice it would be, but before I could answer the surgeon walked in, still in his green operating clothes and silly plastic shoes. We both turned and faced him. As before, he started to talk before he had even finished walking.

"Good news!" he said, "The operation went well. Dan is in intensive care, but this is normal for the first forty-eight hours or so. He will have to stay in hospital for about two weeks. If his body rejects the kidney it will probably happen within that time. Please, do go and see him. I'm going to get cleaned up now, we can talk some more in a while."

"What about the donor? Is he OK?" I asked.

" Oh yes, he's fine."

Before we had time to thank him, he left. We had another big cuddle both knowing it wasn't over yet.

The first thing we saw was a lot of lights flashing and tubes everywhere with blood running through them. The nurse reassured us that it all looked a lot worse than it was. We stayed for a while; me on one side of his bed holding Dan's hand and Dave the other side holding his other hand. The nurses and doctors just carried on doing their stuff as if we weren't even there. Just another's day's work to them I suppose. A little while later the surgeon came in to see Dan. He looked at the monitors, then at the clip board that was hanging on the bottom of Dan's bed, and then he very carefully checked the drip lines that were going into his body.

"OK, fine," he said, "all we can do now is wait. You two should try to get some sleep if you can. We'll see you in the morning. He should be able to talk to you then."

Chapter Five

Dave... The Turning Point

I told Lynn to go back to the room, and get our bits and pieces together to take back home. I needed to get a bit of fresh air and make some phone calls to see if I still had a business left. As I was walking out of intensive care, the door was slightly open to another room and I noticed a nurse attending to a Paki. This got my back up a bit.

"Over here to scrounge an operation on our National Health, is he?" I said to the nurse,

"No!" she snapped back. "He's a donor."

"Who would want a bloody part of him?"

She quickly replied, "We are all the same when our skin is peeled back. If it weren't for him donating one of his kidneys the boy in the other room would probably be dead in a few weeks. I think he's a bloody hero don't you?"

As I walked away I realized what she had just said. They gave my boy a fucking Paki's kidney! Fuck! FUCK! They should fucking ask people before they do things like that! All the emotions of the last few months kicked in and I started to get angry with myself again for being in prison and away from my family. I hate fucking Pakis, and now there is a bit of one inside my son! I put the palm of my hands onto the top of my face, and pressed as hard as I could, to try and push all this shit out of my head. I walked outside.

Before I had any time to think, the same nurse walked up to me, pointing her finger straight at my face,

"You! You!" she kept saying, and then she started to poke me in the chest. "It's your son isn't it? That man risked his life to save your boy, and what about his family if he doesn't make it? How dare you say things like that about such a decent person! And that's more than I can say about you!"

I wanted to smash her face in, then jump all over her body, and crush it into the ground, but I couldn't move. It felt like a hundred people were holding me back; the more I tried to move forward, the more people grabbed me and pulled me back, my legs, my arms, even my face. She just stood there looking at me with disgust. I stared back at her with all the hatred I felt, trying to tear her apart with my mind. Then it hit home!

HE FUCKING SAVED DAN'S LIFE!

I felt physically drained, almost to the point of being sick. That little nurse had really done a number on me! I was three times her size and she had just put me down, beaten me to a pulp, I was fucked, and she knew it. Then she took hold of my hand.

"Are you OK?" she said in a much more forgiving voice. Fuck me! How good are these nurses? They kick you in the bollocks then try to make you better! It's very easy to kick someone you hate in the bollocks, but to then help them get better; well; that takes a very special person. She made sure I was going to be OK, then turned her back on me and walked away, with the confidence that came from knowing she had just brought me down a peg or two.

I stayed in the car park for a while to get myself back together, and try and sort myself out somehow. The rain had stopped now, and the sun was trying its hardest to break through the clouds. I found a couple of old seats under a plastic lean-to, surrounded by a thousand dog ends, and sat down to be on my own. But a few minutes later a couple of porters came out for a quick fag, so I went back up to intensive care. I stood outside the donor's room for a bit; all sorts of shit was going through my head.

What's he like?

Is he married?

What is his family like?

Has he got any children?

Does he have any diseases that he could pass on to Dan?

The door opened and the little nurse came out, she gave me a smile. "Are you sure you're OK?" she said again.

I gave her a half smile back,

"Yes a bit better now, but I need to see the donor."

She shook her head, and snapped at me, "No way, no way, you're not supposed to have any contact with them. I could lose my job over this."

This time I took her hand and said to her, "I really do need to see him; can you please go and ask if it's OK? I won't tell anyone if you let me in there."

She looked at me for a bit. Her head started to shake, slowly this time.

"Christ! What am I thinking!" she sighed. "Stay here. I'll go and ask his wife."

She came back out almost straight away, and said, "It's OK, he's awake now, but don't be too long. I'm going to get her a cup of tea, and when I get back you'd better be out of that room." She was pointing her finger at me again. Normally, if someone did that to me I would break their fingers.

"OK, OK! Pick on someone your own size!" I said.

She gave me a look as if to say 'It's not funny,' and said, "Please hurry up." She walked away, shaking her head and waving her arms about as if she was telling herself off.

I opened the door very slowly and walked in. I'm normally a confident person, but this made me feel very uneasy. His wife was holding his hand. She looked at me, and said, "You must be the father of Dan?"

Fuck! FUCK! I realized they were a family that owned one of the shops on that shit hole of a council estate! She must recognize me; I collect money every week off these people. Bollocks! What do I say now? We just looked at each other; neither of us knew what to say. Then her husband let go of his wife's hand and held it out to hold mine.

"Is your son OK?" he asked.

"Yes he's OK," I said shakily.

What the fuck do you say to a man who has just risked his own life, to try and save your son's? I leant over him and whispered one word in his ear.

"Why?"

He looked at me for a bit, and then said simply,

"Because he needed it."

Fucking hell!! Just like that! Would I have done the same for him? I don't think so. The little nurse was right. He IS a fucking hero!

I looked at his wife. She was so proud of what her husband had just done. I asked if there was anything I could do for them. They looked at each other for a moment; I should have known the answer.

"Could you make sure our two children are OK? They are in our shop on their own."

My heart took another fucking pounding. I wouldn't leave my dog on its own in that place, and the scumbags have been collecting my protection money from them. They would have been told that I was out of prison and would be paying them a visit. I could feel the anger building up inside of me. Not towards these nice people, but towards myself, the scumbags and any other wanker on that shit hole of a council estate who will be taking the piss out of his children while he is in here. I leant over him again, "Your family; don't worry, they will be looked after. I promise." You could see the relief on his face,

"Thank you," he said. He turned to his wife, gave her a little smile and drifted back to sleep. I shook his wife's hand and thanked her again for what her husband had done, and then left them alone before anyone saw me.

Lynn and me went and saw Dan again for a while, until the nurses asked us to leave, to give him time to rest.

"If there are any changes we'll phone you straight away," the nurse promised.

I dropped Lynn home and then went to sort out some very important business. I normally park my car just off the estate and walk in. It lets everyone know I'm still about. All the old faces are still here; nothing ever changes in these places. Scumbags move away or die, and then other scumbags take their place. There were loads of kids of all ages hanging around, kicking anything they could find pretending it was a football;

young girls smoking and swearing and looking like little prostitutes; some old tramps covered in piss, laying on what was left of the benches, probably still drunk from yesterday. Rubbish just dumped in the middle of the street that had now turned into flat paper mash where all the vehicles had run over it. There were always loads of burnt out cars scattered about the place that the joy riders had nicked and set on fire, and then they would throw whatever they could find at the poor firemen who were trying to put the burning cars out.

As always a few yobs, girls as well as boys, were hanging around outside the shop, probably making life hell for the rest of his family, just like my mates and me did when I was that age. I walked inside. There were three skinheads of about 16 or 17 years old, messing about throwing things around the place, and no doubt nicking bits and pieces.

My heart sank, as I saw the two beautiful young girls behind the counter. When he said his kids, I had thought they were boys. He'd left them alone and vulnerable in this shit hole to help my family and me. The girls looked at me. My two scumbags would have told them I was coming to see them today, they guessed who I was, I could see it on their poor little frightened faces. I looked over at the boys. They knew me and I knew them by sight, so they thought it was still OK to keep putting things in their pockets. They were wrong!

Very fucking wrong!

I walked up to the counter and looked at the girls, who were cowering in the corner like a couple of lost puppies. First these three fucking idiots taking the piss, and now me. The girls were holding each other's hands, and they were shitting it.

"Hello, my name's Dave. Your dad has asked me to look after you." No response. I said it again a bit louder, so the boys could hear me as well.

"Here, this is my phone number. If you get any trouble and need my help, please phone me, day or night."

They just nodded slowly in disbelief. I turned to the boys, trying not to scare the girls any more than they already were, if that was possible.

"Right lads time to put it all back."

They sort of started laughing. They know what I'm like with these people, normally I wouldn't give a toss; just collect my money, give whoever was in there nicking stuff a wink, and be on my way. I looked back at the two girls. The youngest one was trying to hide behind her sister and had tears rolling down her face; it brought a lump to my throat. I wanted to pick her up, wrap my arms around her, and give her a big cuddle to try and make her feel safe. It always works with my girls.

Then suddenly my face tensed with pain. It was like a bolt of lightning shooting through my spine and it made me clench my teeth together. What if it was Samantha and Charlotte? In this shop, all alone with these wankers? I couldn't move; even the little nurse started to do her stuff again prodding me with her little finger.

Fuck this! I shook the thought out of my head, I walked over to the biggest one and head butted him as hard as I could. His face split open, the blood pouring out before he fell onto his knees. The other two froze, they didn't know how to react. I leant forward and stuck out my head. I could feel the huge thick muscles of my neck tighten, even the veins in my hands started to bulge out as I rolled them up into tight fists, ready to beat the fuck out of the other two. An inch from their faces I said quietly,

"Put the fucking stuff back!" They did.

"Now go and tell your silly fucking mates that this shop is under my protection. You upset these girls, I will fuck up your body. Take this sack of shit with you, and don't forget to tell your scumbag friends." They couldn't get out quick enough, dragging their half conscious mate with them. I tried to give the girls a friendly smile.

"Remember, day or night, you make sure you phone me. I made a promise to your father that I would look after you. OK?" They gave me a small nod and a false smile.

Now to visit the pubs, just a couple of minutes away. As I was making my way to the first crap hole, I started to wonder why these people settle in places like this. When I really think about it, they have never done me, my sisters or my Mum any harm. They even let Mum have food on the slate when things got tight with money. Their kids were always well behaved and polite. Working was no problem to them, unlike most of the tossers in this shit hole. Why did we hate them so much? Now one of them has saved my son's life. My anger started to focus towards myself again. What the fuck did these people ever do to upset me? Fuck all! That's what! Fuck all!

Some people tried to say 'Hello' to me on the way to the pub; I have no friends on this estate, apart from the two girls in the shop now. What a weird feeling, to be looking after the shop rather than smashing it up!

The pub was only half full but very noisy. The smoke was as thick as fog and looked like it was hanging from the ceiling. Still the same rotten old carpet that looked like it was upside down where all the pile had been worn away, and you could smell the drugs that were burning in the rollups. Same old faces everywhere plus a few new ones. Different bar staff, they never lasted long. The people that knew me (not friends, they just knew me,) were beginning to feel uneasy. The loud talking now turned into nervous whispers; the cigarettes were now being sucked a lot harder, as if each suck was going to be their last!

Nearly every time I've been in this pub someone had been taught a lesson. I walked over to the bar.

"Where's the manager?" I asked. The fat and ugly old peroxide bird said, "I'll get him for you," past the cigarette that was hanging out of the side of her mouth.

Fuck me it was only 'Fingers!' His little face looked like he had just seen a fucking ghost!

"I, I, I don't want any trouble Dave," he stuttered.

"The mike on the stage, does it work?" I asked him,

"Yes" he said, with a look of 'what the hell is he up to?' I told him to switch it on for me. I looked around the pub at them all for a bit, then tapped the top of the mike to make sure it was working. I could see them all thinking, 'what the fuck? Is he going to give us a song?' I've used a microphone loads of times up on a stage before, to get the punters out of the clubs at the end of the night, so it didn't bother me standing up here.

"The people that own the food shop just around the corner, they are friends of mine, and I don't want them to get any aggro." Disbelief on all of their faces, along with a couple of shouts;

"OK Dave, you're having a laugh!"

"OK, let's put it another way then. If any of you fucking scumbags cause trouble for that family, I will smash you, your kids, your wife and your fucking house to pieces!"

Complete silence.

I looked around at the new faces for any reaction. There was a bunch of guys sitting at a table, an up and coming gang by the look of them. One of them was staring hard at me; he was a big fucker, maybe their leader. I focused on him, but he soon turned his head away. He was probably trying to get some respect from his little gang by staring at me for a bit. If any one of them had said something, I would have jumped all over his fucking head, and anyone that was sitting with him.

I told Fingers to give me an orange juice, and then I sat at the bar for a while to give them time to react. Nothing. Fuck them all! I did the same in the other crap hole pub. Fuck them all as well! I went to check on the girls again. This time I got a response, not much, but a least they understood that I would be around for them, which sort of cheered them both up a bit. I told them they should be very proud of their father for what he has done, it was a very brave thing to do; they looked at each other, smiled and then had a little cuddle. "I must go now. Make sure you put my number safe, and if you get any problems, day or night, make sure you phone me."

They still couldn't take it all in but at least I got a couple of proper smiles this time.

I started walking back to my car, a few more people tried to say 'Hello' to me, but with all this emotional shit going on over the last three days, I couldn't even be bothered to turn my head and tell them to fuck off!

I made a quick visit to the office to see Big Steve and Kate, which turned out to be a long visit, to get a run down on what places needed to be sorted out, but the boys had done a good job. Just a couple of doormen that will need to have their asses kicked; as always, when the cat's away the silly mice will always fuck about!

When I got home Lynn was asleep on the couch. A note for me on the table saying she had spoken to the hospital and that Dan was fine, and that my Mum had phoned from Canada to say the airports were still closed, the snowstorms were getting worse, but she hopes to see you soon. I put a blanket over her, gave her a little kiss on the cheek, and went to bed. We both managed to get a good night's sleep.

A bit of breakfast in the morning, then it was back up to the hospital. Dan was still very weak of course but doing really well; no complications yet, but the donor, whose name I found out was Ravi, wasn't doing so well. He had picked up an infection, even with all the antibiotic shit they were pumping into him, he wasn't getting any better. I asked the nurse if he was going to be OK. She just looked at me, and started biting at her bottom lip; I knew what she was thinking, that it didn't look good for him.

We stayed up at the hospital for most of the day, but there wasn't a lot we could do except wait. One of the nurses suggested it might be a good idea to take Samantha and Charlotte out for a walk down by the river to feed the ducks, as it's only five minutes away. We were probably getting in their way and asking too many questions, it was a polite way of saying 'can you please get out from under our feet and let us get on with our job', and I think that she might have been right.

It turned out to be a lovely afternoon. The girls were taking everything really well and were both so positive. All that Lynn and me could think about was all the things that could go wrong, but all they were thinking about was what we could all do when Dan was better. It was nice to spend some time with them away from all the hospital stuff, and it did take our minds off things for a short while.

After the ducks had been fattened up a bit with four loaves of your finest uncut whole meal, we found a little café. Lynn and me had a cup of tea, the girls had a 99 ice cream with extra flakes, and then we headed back to the hospital. Nothing had changed. Dan was asleep and the nurse told us it would be best if we all went home to try to get some rest as well.

As I was driving home, I couldn't stop thinking about Ravi's girls in the shop on their own. Fuck it! I hit the side of my head a couple of times with the inside of my hand, why hadn't I got their phone number? I could give them a ring to make sure they were OK instead of worrying about them all the bloody time!

It had been four days since the transplant and Dan's skin colour had gone back to normal. They told us before the operation, that when this happens it's a good sign that Dan's body had not rejected the kidney.

Ravi wasn't getting any better; it turned out that he was allergic to the antibiotics they'd been giving him, the poor sod, he should have been thinking about going home by now. Whenever I went to see Dan I made sure I spoke to Ravi when he was able to talk, or to his wife, Meana, to reassure them that things were fine at the shop and their girls were safe. Fuck me! Anything could happen on that shit hole, I kept thinking to myself.

Ravi's girls came to visit their dad at the hospital every night after they had finished work. If I wasn't around at the same time I made sure Lynn asked them if they were both OK. Christ! We were all becoming friends! Even Charlotte and Samantha started to hang around with Ravi's girls when they met at the hospital.

Lenny and the two Franks had done a good job looking after the doors while I was away. Lenny had bit of trouble when some businessmen approached him on the door one night to see if he would work for them. They asked to see his boss. Lenny told them I was out of town for a bit, which everyone knows normally means prison!

Then there was some trouble at the club a couple of nights in a row. They were testing him to see how much bottle he had, and if he could hold it together without the boss around. They were probably seeing if they could take over the door with their own staff. Lenny and the Franks would never back down. Plus I'd still been able to organize some stuff from prison by phone. As soon as I got a chance, they would be getting a visit from me, just in case they decided to have another go. It's even more important that the door work stays solid now that there's no more money coming in from Ravi's shop; the little nurse put a stop to that!

My mobile rang, it was one of Ravi's girls.

"Hello Dave, sorry to trouble you but we're having some problems at the shop. I'm a bit worried as he said they would be back."

"I'll be there as quick as I can." The two scumbags that used to collect the money for me are trying to get it for themselves. I used the money on my family but these fuckers would put it in their arms or up their noses. I was no better than them when I collected it, but things have changed now.

No time for walking this time. I drove my car right up to the shop front. Scumbag one was standing outside. He didn't recognize the car or me at first, but as soon as it clicked, he was away on his toes. For a scumbag junkie he could really fucking fly! I knew where I could find him.

I went into the shop and got a bit of a surprise. Scumbag two was just standing there on his own. He looked me straight in the eyes. He was as high as a kite, and probably thought I was Scumbag one coming in for some bloody crisps or something!

I looked at Jema, that's not her name but it was as close as I could get to her real name, and it always makes her smile. But not today, she looked petrified.

"Where's your big sister? Is she OK?"

No response, just those huge terrified eyes.

I took another couple of steps forward and looked over the counter out to the back of the shop, and what I saw out there made my blood boil. Another fucker! He had a knife and what looked like the day's takings in his other hand. I had to be very careful; these fuckers on the gear will do anything to get their fix for the day. A knife can do some real damage very quickly, and he was so close to Jema's sister.

We just stood there looking at each other for a bit. Scumbag two was trying to take in what was happening, Anija was looking at me for help, and she didn't know what to do. My body was pumping with adrenalin. My fists were clenched so tight they felt like lumps of rock. Then he said,

"All I want is the money."

"Then take the fucking money and go," I said to him.

I moved to the side to give him some room, and make him feel like he had a way out.

He moved slowly away from Anija, one little step at a time, then through the gap in the counter and past Jema. One more step onto the shop floor, and then he turned and pointed the knife at me! Big mistake! I took a quick step to the right, landed one punch and he was on the floor before the money had time to float down.

Silly bollocks Scumbag two had come to life now. Too late! I grabbed his head and pulled it down as hard as I could, lifting my knee at the same time. Five or six should do it, breaking some different part of his face each time they met!

I collected the money together and gave it back to the girls, who were still hiding round the back. Brave little things, putting up with all this shit.

Knife man was trying to get up, so I dragged him outside by his head and around the back, away from the shop, by some bins. I bent right down to his ear,

"Can you hear me?" His blood-covered Afro nodded a yes.

"This is for what you've just done."

I picked up his arm and put it against my knee, one hand either side and pulled. He screamed. I pulled harder. He screamed louder. Nice and slow, nothing quick for this fucker! His body arched up with the pain. One more tug, and he fainted as the bone broke. I then did the same to the other arm. Fuck him! I dragged the other junkie out of the shop, and parked him with his mate.

I cleaned up the mess for the girls, helped them to pull the shutters down, and made sure they were going to be all right, and then I set of to find scumbag one. He was standing in the corner of the pub with his back to me. I picked up a glass ashtray on my way over to him. The vermin he was drinking with never said a word but their body language told him something bad was going to happen. He was half turned around just as the ashtray connected with his face and he went straight down on his back. The vermin all took a step back, you could tell none of them wanted a part of this, (which was just as well, as the mood I was in all of their faces would have been smelling of old cigarette butts!) I grabbed him by his neck, forcing my thumb behind his windpipe and lifted his head up ready for another beating.

"They made me do it!" he gargled, through a mouth full of blood.

Well, well! It seemed a new family had just moved onto the estate. I knew my two scumbags didn't have the bollocks to do it on their own. He told me where they lived, just before the ashtray came and done its bit again. He won't like what he sees in the mirror each morning. Fuck him! Nobody likes a grass anyway. They'll probably be going through his pockets as soon as I've gone!

A quick look around the pub, they wouldn't know whose face I remembered and whose I didn't. They knew I would find out if anyone mentioned my name. I told them what would happen, they don't fucking listen.

By the time I found the new family's flat I was wound up even more.

No knocking this time. I ran at the door and hit it smack in the middle with my shoulder, hoping it would only take one go, but the whole fucking frame came off as well! There was no response at first, then some shouting from inside one of the rooms. They were from Africa, or somewhere like that. Two of them came running out at me, screaming at the top of their voices, it sounded like some sort of voodoo shit, and they were trying to put up a fight. One even got a punch in; it was to be his last for a long time.

After knocking them both out, I picked up an old bowling ball off the floor. Their hands were facing the wrong way by the time I stopped hitting them.

Another one came jumping down the stairs with a baseball bat. His bloodshot eyes were nearly popping out of his head because he was so high on drugs, the silly fucker! I snatched the bat out of his hand then rammed his head into the corner of the metal dinning table, splitting the whole side of his face open from top to bottom. I stood over him for a bit, watching the blood pour out. His cheek looked sort of like an old banana skin, but a gooey red one, and then I broke the bat over his legs.

I stood still ready for some more drug-crazed fuckers to come flying out of the woodwork, but all that was left was a big fat wrinkled old woman with half her teeth missing. She wobbled out of the kitchen with a big shiny silver knife in one hand and some beads in the other, shouting some old shit, probably trying to put a spell on me! She was so fucking ugly; one punch straight in the face lifted her off her feet and knocked out some more teeth! Fuck her and her family!

I walked around the house smashing everything to pieces. It had to be a clear warning; don't fuck with me; I always do what I say I'm going to do. Even when we are working the doors some people just don't listen. It's only a smack in the mouth that they understand, fucking idiots!

Four weeks passed really quickly. My Mum and sisters had come and gone. The word soon got around the council estate that I was out of prison, and looking after things again. The girls haven't had any more trouble since my last visit.

Dan was coming on in leaps and bounds, and after four weeks, he was allowed to come home, which was fantastic, so a visit to the beach with Dan's new kidney was called for! Every day he just seemed to get better and better, and was nearly back to his old self. It was great to have the whole family back together again.

Ravi was still having problems; he wasn't getting any worse, just not getting any better. Either Lynn or me went to see him every day, and all he wanted to hear was that his daughters were OK. We never took Dan to see Ravi. It would have been too much for both of them.

I even took an Indian on my team to look after the doors. Who would have thought that could happen six months ago? Not me! Baz wasn't your average Indian, not your turban wearing type, and he wasn't that religious, but he was built like a JCB, and none of it fat! He was good to have at the clubs where a lot of young Indian people gathered. Baz was able to calm them down a lot better and much quicker than the other doormen, but if they did get out of hand, there was no hesitation; he would get it sorted out very quickly. Baz wasn't his whole name. It would have taken ages to keep saying his name in full, and he preferred Baz anyway.

After the club we were working at had closed, and most of the punters had gone home, I pulled him to one side away from the other doormen, and told him about Ravi, the shop and the girls. He didn't say anything at first, but as it began to sink in, his head tilted back a bit as if he was going to head butt me, and his eyes started to bulge out of his face. I thought he was going to try and sort me out. No chance, but Baz is a family man, and it made him really angry. We stood there looking at each other for a bit, he still wasn't saying anything, but I could tell he was thinking about the girls as if they were his own. They do like to help each other out these people. Not like a lot of English people. Turn your back and they would have the shirt off it, then everything they could carry from your house, and nick your car to carry it all away in, if they could!

"No problem," he said, as his eyes went back into their sockets and his big square head started to relax again. "It's not too far from me." I shook his hand and thanked him.

I took Baz up the hospital to meet Ravi, and told him that Baz would be calling into the shop as well to make sure the girls were OK.

Ravi slowly rolled on to his side and reached out his arm, he put his hand into Baz's then put his other hand over the top, and slowly shook it for about two minutes, talking to Baz in his own language.

It was the longest thank you I've ever heard, but it all ended with everyone smiling, especially Meana.

A few more weeks went by, and Dan was well enough to do some off road driving that I had promised him we would do just before he had the transplant, to try and cheer him up a bit. He was so excited. The school was a couple of hours drive away on a farm. It was great to spend a bit of time with my family, away from the concrete jungle we live in.

The people at the driving school were very friendly and made a great effort to make us feel comfortable right from the start, even the girl who showed us where to park the car did it with a warm smile.

We walked into a big old barn that looked like it was about to fall over, but inside it was fantastic, with all the big wooden beams exposed and a great big open fire burning right at the end, although it still wasn't all that warm.

"First things first!" the guy said, "help yourself to as much tea and coffee as you like, and there's plenty of fizzy crap drinks for the younger ones!"

Everyone had a smile to themselves at his honesty! After Dan and me had signed in, Lynn and the girls headed off with some other women to the part of the farm with all the animals and lots of other stuff to keep the family entertained while the boys go off to play with their toys! Dan and me, six men and two other boys around the same age as Dan all climbed onto a big old wooden cart, pulled by a tractor to the off road track, which was away from the main farm.

We were all from built up areas, so it was great to be out in the fresh air, if you ignored the smell of the cows shit! Even before we'd got to the farm, my car's air vents had given us a taste of the country life! We'd all started to blame each other for letting one off, the five of us couldn't stop laughing, and from then on I knew it was going to be a great day!

The three boys loved being pulled by the big rusty old tractor. Four of the older guys were very posh, and you could tell they all had a bit of money. I didn't really get on with people like that. They would normally be the ones in the clubs flashing their wads about, and buying over-priced fizzy wine with a Champagne label on it, getting too drunk, and then starting something they couldn't finish. They were a bit loud for my liking, pretending to be cowboys with lassoes, trying to catch the cows as we went past them; you could have walked up to the bloody cows and tied a rope around their necks, they were so tame!

It turned out that they were all very nice, just letting off steam and glad to get away from all the back-stabbers they worked with. Two of them owned a couple of casinos, and they said any time I wanted to go, just give them a ring and they'd get Lynn and me in for some V.I.P. treatment! The other two big old fellers were a couple of old builders from north London! I could tell they were enjoying the ride too, by the little smiles on their faces, although I bet they wouldn't admit it! Me too!

The first hour was all about safety and how to drive the vehicles, which started to get a bit boring, but as soon as we put our racing overalls on, and got into the cars, we were all excited again. It wasn't about speed, but how to get these four-wheel drive land rovers through three or four feet of mud, and up and over some very steep and slippery hills. Dan picked it up really quickly for someone who had never driven before, and was soon driving the car on his own, with the instructor next to him of course. We both loved it and the whole day turned out to be great fun.

Baz kept to his word. Three or four times a week he would pop into the shop, sometimes staying there for a couple of hours just talking to the girls. Good! The longer he stayed, the more people would see him. Even with Baz doing his bit I would still visit the shop just as often as before, and when Ravi gets out of hospital my help will always be there for him and his family.

Sometimes Baz and me would turn up at the same time, have a chat and a cup of tea, and, of course, take the piss out of Jema and Anija! I would often get their names mixed up, but they would just laugh, and do the same to me, take the piss and call me Baz, and call Baz Dave! It was great to see them so relaxed when we were there, having a bit of fun and not worrying about their dad or the scumbags around this place all the time.

Baz was a very hard man, but he had a gentle and caring side to him as well. I saw a different person when he was around children, he almost turned into one himself, what with some of the stupid things he would say and do! But as soon as someone walked through the shop door he would stop talking and check out the customer to see if they were a threat to the girls.

If it were scum his body language would change to 'You don't fuck with me or these girls.' If it was an old lady he would go straight into welcome mode and make her feel at ease; you can't learn that, it's just what he's made of. I liked Baz, he was a gentleman, and he loved his family, and would do anything for them. The more Indian people I got to know, the more I realized, they are no different from us, all they want to do is go to work and earn enough money to look after their families. I've come into contact with a couple of scumbag Indians on the estate that had to be sorted out, but it was probably the council estate that turned them into scumbags. Fuck them! Baz was with me on that one.

Everyone got the same chance, some people go for it, and most of the people on here don't. Some can't see it, and most don't give a shit. Then there are ones who try to take from everyone else. Bollocks to them!

Baz, with his family, Jema and Anija and their Mum have all been round to our house a few times now. Samantha and Charlotte are younger than Ravi's girls but they all get on so well. Baz has seven kids of all ages, and all over the place, but they are so well behaved and polite, you can't help but like them. His wife, like Lynn, loves her kids so much, and you can see they all love her. Baz doesn't stop smiling when his family are all together and happy, a very proud man.

We became very good friends over the next few months. We even talked about opening up the off-licence next to Ravi's shop together. There would be no shortage of customers on that place!

I wasn't getting money from the shop any more and it sounded like a good idea, but trying to find someone to work in that shit hole who wouldn't nick the money and drink all the drink wouldn't be easy.

Then came the phone call we'd all been waiting for! Ravi was well enough to come home! The poor sod had been in hospital for months. He was a lot better, still very weak, but he couldn't wait to be home with his family. The hospital said a nurse would do a home visit every other day to make sure he was OK.

So much has gone on since I have been out of prison; the girls have changed school again; so more bloody uniforms! Dan has got a moped, which I'm not very happy with; and he's been going around with some older kids I'm not too sure about, but I know I have to try and let him go and do his own thing. One minute he was dying, now he just wants to do all the things he thought he would never be able to do.

From day one the doctors have said that getting a new kidney isn't a 100% cure, it just gives you a bit more time, and then its back on the waiting list for another one. It wasn't easy for Lynn and me to talk about this;

God knows what it must feel like to Dan? It's so difficult to tell a teenager to slow down, you've got plenty of time, and you are so young! How do you tell that to someone who's been through what Dan has?

The day had finally come! A big 'welcome home' party had been arranged at Ravi's house; once again, all his friends and family came together to help Meana and his girls to make it a very special time. Lynn, Charlotte and Samantha made lots of cakes and every woman who turned up brought at least three plates of food! Others brought the extra tables and chairs needed, and a bloody great marquee appeared in the garden! All the kids were blowing up balloons and trying to tie knots in the ends, but mostly they just let them go, so they would fly around the garden making funny noises! Baz showed them all how to put a small coin in the end, so now when they let go, the balloons shot around the garden making a screaming noise. Thanks a lot, Baz! Still, it made him laugh, until he got a bollocking from his wife; now that was funny, watching big old Baz getting told off like a naughty little school kid! I held my hand up so Baz could see it, and then smacked the top of it with my other hand as if to say 'who's a naughty boy then!' He nodded his head and mimed 'ha, ha!'

It still feels strange having Indians as friends. Some of my old mates can't get their heads around it, but because they know what Ravi has done for Dan, they sort of accept it.

Jema and Anija had made a banner reading;

'WELCOME HOME DADDY!'

It hung across the front of the house. They were so excited to be having the family back together again.

Everything was ready, with the women still running around in circles trying to make it even better! All the children were playing a game together. Baz was sipping on his usual glass of water, and trying to stay out of trouble, and the hot sun, but smiling from ear to ear, watching his kids laughing. That's all he wanted in life. It made me smile as well, but all I could think of was where the fuck was Dan, and where the fuck was the ambulance?

"I'm going to ring the hospital," I said to Lynn.

The number was already programmed into my phone. I pressed speed dial, and it went straight to the ward where Ravi had been. Two rings and someone answered. I was impressed!

"Hello my name's Dave, a friend of Ravi Patel. We were told the ambulance would drop him home about three o'clock. It's now nearly five o'clock and there's no sign of him." The nurse didn't answer me but I could tell she was still there.

"Can you hear me?" I asked.

"Yes" she said, "but I need to talk to one of Ravis' family."

This got my back up. "Just tell me if he has left the hospital yet."

"I really need to speak to one of his family," she repeated.

I was just going to give her a proper mouthful when a police car slowly pulled up outside.

'Oh bollocks, now what?' I said to myself. You never know what to expect in my line of business. Is one of my doormen in trouble? Or have I been caught on camera again bashing up a punter? I'm really getting the hump now, no fucking ambulance, no Dan, now these two clowns turn up. Lynn moved closer to me. She had been in these situations before. They usually ended with me getting carted away. Sometimes I would come home the same night. Sometimes it would be a couple of months, depending on the evidence.

We all stood there looking at the coppers and they just sat there looking at us. After about 30 seconds they slowly got out of the car. The one closest to us waited for the other copper to walk around the car and meet him before they started to walk down the garden path. No rush, very calm. I had seen one of them loads of times, he normally did the night shift and always stopped for a chat if I was out in front of a club. Not a bad copper, as coppers go.

I cut the hospital off my mobile. Something wasn't right with these two and I was ready for trouble. Fuck them! The way I was feeling, they can have it. Then I thought 'Why only two of them?' They had no chance against me. I am well known by the police so there are always at least five or six to come and get me. I wouldn't normally give them any trouble, all depending on what mood I was in. My heart started to pump like mad. I moved closer to Lynn, her hand slid into mine, as we both realized they didn't have their hats on. That only means one thing.

Bad news.

Just as I started to think things might be getting back to normal, they couldn't have got any worse. You never know what's around the next corner. You think life could not be better, then some one doesn't just pull the rug from under your feet, they take the hole fucking floor!

Everything around me seemed to stop moving. I couldn't speak, and all I could hear was the coppers' footsteps walking towards us. Lynn's hand tightened around mine, her body leaning into me and she tilted her head onto my shoulder. We just stood there as they got closer and closer, as if it was happening in slow motion. They were now about three or four feet away, and I felt my body start to shake. I gritted my teeth together, ready for the words every parent dreads.

The copper spoke, "Are you Meana Patel?"

No one said a word. After about ten seconds he repeated it. That's when I realized he wasn't looking or talking to us. Everything around me started to move again. The noise from all the kids playing in the garden slowly got louder and louder until my silent world got back to normal. Everyone looked at Meana.

"Are you Meana Patel?"

A couple of her friends put their arms around her shoulders and answered for her.

"Yes."

"I'm so very sorry," the copper said quietly. "The ambulance that was bringing your husband home has been involved in an accident with a drunk driver. We are very sorry, but Ravi has been killed. We have the driver of the other vehicle at the station."

Silence.

Meana turned around and looked at her daughters. They hadn't taken in what had been said, they didn't want to hear it.

Meana looked up at the 'Welcome Home' sign for a while, it was moving slowly in the hot breeze. It had looked fantastic when it first went up, now it's just a lonely piece of old paper, with no more use. Then she dropped to her knees, holding her head in her hands and started praying. Jema and Anija stood frozen to the spot as tears started to roll down their cheeks.

Lynn put her arms around them both and cried with them.

I looked at Baz. His smile had gone, he looked confused and his hands had come out of his pockets, his body had gone into work mode. No one knew what to say or do. Baz and me have been in some violent situations together and both knew what to do without saying a word to each other. This time, we were looking at each other and I knew what he was thinking and he knew what I was thinking, 'what the fuck do we do now?'

The copper said quietly, "We need someone to identify the body." No reaction from anyone. The copper put his hand on my shoulder and said again, "We need someone to come to the hospital to identify the body." I knew this copper, and he knew why I was here..

Baz walked over to me and said, "I'll go mate, and you stay here." He knew I was fucked.

Baz got into the back of the cops' car. As they slowly drove away, Baz turned around and looked out of the back window. He gave me one of his nods. This time I knew exactly what he meant.

I told Lynn to look after things here while I go to the police station to find out what had happened. Lynn is good when the shit hits the fan, she's had plenty of practice with my mates and me, but she did tell me to hurry back this time.

I walked to my car, thinking 'what a fucking mess.' My body was still in shock and my mind was all over the place. The car was parked just around the corner out of sight of everyone. I sat there for a while trying to pull myself together, but it wasn't long before the anger started to take over. I have had to deal with drunks all my life. Taking the piss out of me, trying to fight me or stab me; they all paid the price. This fucker has done more than all of them put together. I knew what had to be done with that one quick look from Baz through the back window of the cops' car.

I started up the engine, and drove off without going round the front of the house again. Too much shit happening back there. On the way to the police station I was saying to myself over and over to just get a name, the boys will do the rest. It might even be a woman. Fuck them, whoever it was they are going to get very badly hurt.

I walked into the police station. The little pencil neck behind the counter gave me the right fucking hump straight away with his silly fucking attitude.

"The drunk driver who killed the man in the ambulance; is he here?" I said.

"We can't give out that information," he snapped back, and then he carried on with his meaningless paperwork as if I wasn't there. I looked at the little shit for a bit, trying very hard not to lose my rag. Then I asked him if I could find out any more info about what happened.

He looked at me with an even bigger attitude, and said, "I told you the first time, we can't give out that sort of information."

He thought he was untouchable behind that counter, but with all the attitude in the world I could tell he was wary of me, his body language told me that. They are taught to try and cover up their fear to give them an edge over the person they are dealing with or going to arrest, but this silly fucker was trying to do it with some serious attitude, and it wasn't working on me.

I leant forward over the counter, and put my face right into his. "Just tell me if he is here you little tosser, or I'll have a look myself."

He jumped back and pushed a button, then all fucking hell broke out. Coppers running everywhere, I was surrounded by them. I recognized some of them; they were a bit worried about what was going to happen next. I could see it by the way they were looking at each other, and the way they were fidgeting.

Then a voice from the past:

"Dave! Take it easy mate, don't do anything silly, we're both on the same side with this one."

I stared at them all; they could see that I was ready to go at any time.

"I need to talk to you on your own," said the copper. He was all right, this one. An old school copper, we sort of got on OK. Not the best of friends, but we had a bit of respect for each other. He knew how hard my job was, and I knew how hard his job was with all these fucking do-gooders about. Just as I started to calm down and think to myself 'don't do anything stupid,' out of the corner of my eye, I saw someone in handcuffs being led away.

One of the silly young coppers whispered to his mate, "That's the drunk driver of the other car."

My eyes rolled back into my head and I exploded like a fucking mad man, taking down one copper after another. There was no stopping me until I got to him. They tried to get him out. I was getting closer and closer. More head butts, fists, biting, and lots of blood splashing all over the place. The bastards were hitting me with everything they could, but I felt no pain. The more they hit me the stronger I got. I will tear them to fucking bits if I have to.

The prisoner had his back to me and was trying desperately to get away, but the silly fucking copper couldn't find the right key for the door. Closer and closer, another pig smashed up and out of the way. They found the key and started to open the door, the prisoner wasn't saying a word, but I could see he was so fucking desperate to get away. They had him half out of the door when I grabbed him by the hair, and pulled it as hard as I could. His head bent backwards and he fell back into the room.

He screamed out, "DAD! Dad, I'm sorry! Please don't hurt me!"

I froze.

For a split second I was back in the hospital car park with the little nurse prodding me, and a hundred people holding me back. It gave them time to grab me and bring me down. I was lying in a pool of blood and sweat. Five or six coppers were on top of me, screaming at their mates to help them, pushing their knees into my spine as hard as they could, and all I could do was move my head just enough to see Dan. He had tears rolling down his face and was shaking with fear.

"What the fuck is he doing in here?" I screamed at them.

One of the coppers bent down to my ear and said, "He's the drunk driver that killed Ravi."

THE END

Lightning Source UK Ltd.
Milton Keynes UK
UKOW02f1914231215

265335UK00001B/5/P